Five Russian Dog Stories

Five Russian Dog Stories

translated by Anthony Briggs

Published by Hesperus Press Limited
28 Mortimer Street, London W1W 7RD
www.hesperuspress.com

This translation first published by Hesperus Press Limited, 2012

Translation © Anthony Briggs, 2012

Designed and typeset by Fraser Muggeridge studio
Printed in Jordan by Jordan National Press

ISBN: 978-184391-365-8

CONTENTS

INTRODUCTION

'Sir, I *prefer* dogs.'

These words were spoken some years ago across the bar at the oldest pub in England, The George at Norton St Philip, near Bath, purveyors of the old familiar juice since 1397. A friend and I had asked the owner whether he would accept dogs into his stone-flagged room; this was his response. On another occasion in the same area, our three Giant Schnauzers were each treated to a slice of hot beef carried from the kitchen by a landlord who, without claiming a preference for dogs, also loved and admired them.

These pleasant recollections are not exceptional. Many people love their dogs with extravagance, sometimes comparing them favourably to any humans they have known. To take a famous example, Lord Byron, having lost a Newfoundland to rabies in 1808, claimed that this animal, Boatswain, possessed 'all the Virtues of Man without his Vices'. He went on,

> To mark a friend's remains these stones arise.
> I never had but one, and here he lies.

The monument, the inscription and a portrait of the dog can still be seen at Newstead Abbey.

Other famous people have had memorable associations with the species. Odysseus' beloved Argos died from joy when his long-awaited master returned. Greyfriars Bobby watched over his master's grave from 1858 to 1872. Great men as varied as Sir Isaac Newton, Sir Walter Scott and Sir Winston Churchill are still linked in biographical memory with their dogs Diamond, Hamlet and Rufus.

We have every reason to hold dogs in high esteem if only to acknowledge their role in our emergence as a successful species, which some historians have described as indispensable. Approximately 150,000 years ago modern humans walked out of Africa and spread out. DNA studies suggest that this was also the period during which dogs began to split off from the wolves. Eventually dogs moved in on human communities, from which they have never retreated or been in danger of expulsion. There comes a time when dog and man can be shown to be inseparable, perhaps as recently as 18,000 years ago, and the symbiotic relationship, begun in the Stone Age, certainly helped us through the transition from our days of hunting and gathering to those of settled farming folk in the Neolithic period. Dogs led the field in domestication; other animals would follow into human society, but only after another 5–6,000 years, by which time our dogs were fully prepared to help with the herding and guarding. It was when we sat down with dogs that we could start to build the kind of civilisation that we now enjoy.

But there is another important factor to take note of, one that will not show up in archaeological or DNA evidence. This is affinity. As one historian puts it, 'The fact is, people like dogs, and *vice versa*.' There always has been more to the man-dog relationship than practical advantage. We enjoy being together, and we trust each other. Fifteen thousand years ago we fell in love, the one species with the other, and we still love each other in countless examples until death us do part. This, rather than any idea of usefulness, is what accounts for the affectionate attitudes mentioned above, whereby people sometimes set dogs on the same level as fellow-humans.

In England there are ten million domestic dogs – an astonishing figure when you think how many of us are squeezed into towns. A third of all households share space and time with a dog, and nearly all the dogs are loved to distraction. The landlord of The George was not announcing anything unusual; most of us have a preference for dogs, if not over humans at least over all other animals.

As our oldest friends, dogs were bound to insinuate themselves into our culture, and, sure enough, they turn up at the earliest stages of recorded art. Cave paintings from 10–15,000 years ago show hunting expeditions with the dead animal on display along with men and dogs. Dogs came into their own during the ancient civilisations of Egypt and China, and since then they have been ubiquitous. Pieter Brueghel's *Hunters in the Snow* (1565) may be taken as an iconic descendant of the cave-paintings, linking the same partnership and the same tradition over many long millennia, though dogs in modern art are by no means limited to hunting scenes. They fit naturally into many an indoor and outdoor scene, and Byron's commissioning of Boatswain's portrait was not unusual.

It is in literature that dogs make good. Brave hounds appear in every ancient myth, national saga and narrative poem, and in modern times writers of fiction have extended the depiction to include every dog you can think of. The dogs of literature come in all breeds, shapes and sizes. Cerberus (three-headed guardian of Hades) and Sirius (the Dog star, with a most impressive Latin name: *Alpha Canis Majoris*) go way back into myth and legend; from more recent times you may recall Jack London's *White Fang*, Jerome K. Jerome's Montmorency from *Three Men in a Boat*, or Conan Doyle's *Hound of the Baskervilles*; from childhood, Peter Pan's Nana, Toto from *The Wizard of Oz*, and the Famous Five's Timmy; everybody remembers Bill Sikes's dog in *Oliver Twist* (for those with failing memory his name was Bull's-Eye). One can't forget Launce's Crab ('the sourest natured dog that lives') from Shakespeare's *Two Gentlemen of Verona*, or King Lear's remembered dogs, Trey, Blanche, Sweetheart (canine images of his three daughters); and surely the heroine of *Lassie Come Home* (1943) will never be forgotten – and she came from a novel. These are just some of the stellar performers. Innumerable novels and stories have walk-on parts for dogs, though they attract little attention because it is so natural for us to see them in human company.

Given the reputation enjoyed by the British for both literary achievement and love of animals, we could be expected to lead the field in bringing these interests together. Strong as we are in this area, however, we seem to be outclassed by the Russians, certainly in relation to dogs. The great Russian writers established a rich tradition, not yet exhausted, of bringing dogs into their stories and poems. Twenty years ago I had no trouble in finding twenty writers who had done this, and determining the names of at least fifty individual literary dogs. The most recent was Georgiy Vladimov's *Good Old Ruslan*, a title which is meant to resonate against one of the stories in this collection. This short novel, which describes the decline and death of a Gulag guard dog after the closure of his labour camp, contains a bitter critique of Stalinist totalitarianism; written in the 1960s, it was regarded as un-publishable until the mid-1970s, and came out in Russia for the first time only in 1989.

The first dogs in Russian literature were those who appeared in fables, a genre first popularised by Aesop and imitated in France by La Fontaine during the seventeenth century. These verse stories of talking animals (including many a dog) are intended to demonstrate human failings and follies. Those of Aesop, written 2,000 years before La Fontaine, were themselves inherited, as we can see, from Egyptian papyri dating back a further 1,000 years. We have included one or two of these Russian fables in this collection, for amusement and illustration. Chronologically, they should all have appeared together before the stories, but we have offset them in the interests of diversity. There is one formal feature of these poems that may be worth looking out for. To avoid tedium, the line-lengths are imaginatively varied from one foot to as many as six, and the rhymes do not coincide with line-length; a short line may rhyme with a very long one. We have copied the rhyme-schemes and line-lengths so that the unpredictability of the originals is preserved.

The greatest Russian dog stories are not second-rate literature; they are written by the big Russian writers. For instance, turn to Tolstoy's *War and Peace* and *Anna Karenina* if you want to excerpt for your own pleasure some of the best writing about animals. In the former (Volume II, Part Four, Chapters 4–6) you will read some of Tolstoy's most vigorous prose, based on intimate knowledge of country life, as he describes the most famous wolf-hunt in literature. This is writing of astonishing accuracy and involvement, and the main participants are dogs. The successful hunt is followed by an equally exciting episode later in the day, in which Nikolay Rostov races his beloved and priceless Milka against Yerza, recently exchanged for three whole families of Russian house-serfs, and Rugay, a third dog who cost his owner nothing. We shall not say whether any of them gets the hare. All of this goes to the root of the man-dog partnership, taking us back to where it began, in co-operation for the hunt.

In *Anna Karenina* (Part VI, Chapters 10–11), there is a third form of hunting: shooting with dogs. The best bit of this outing is not just the triumph of patience over disappointment, when a good day follows a bad one, but in the intimate relationship between Dmitri Levin and his dog, Laska. The dog is a wiser old bird than Levin thinks. Part-way through the bad day Laska realises that nothing is going well, and it is not worth trying too hard. In a moment of sharp insight, the author describes how she picks up her master's mood – she realises nothing is going to come right.

> A snipe flew up from under the dog. Levin fired. But it was not his day: he missed, and when he went to look for the one that he had killed, he did not find that either. He crawled all through the sedge, but *Laska did not believe that he had killed the bird*, and, when he sent her to search for it, *she pretended she was looking for it but didn't really do so.* [Author's italics]

Could it be that Tolstoy has exaggerated the dog's powers of perception? Is this an example of the false attribution of human characteristics to animals – of anthropomorphism? Dog-lovers will deny this, recognising this scene as typical of a dog's sensitivity, resourcefulness and willingness to please.

But we cannot digress further into the work of the great novelists. Suffice it to say that Fyodor Dostoyevsky is also good on dogs, on a smaller scale but over a wider range to include mongrels and scruffy prison dogs. So is Gogol, so are most of the great literary figures. But the best of them all is Ivan Turgenev, the author of the most successful story in this collection.

Ivan Turgenev and Mumu

Ivan Turgenev was the author of six novels, including *Fathers and Children* (1862); a series of sketches from rural life, *A Hunter's Notes* (1852); and more than thirty stories of varying length and quality. Nearly all of these works have dogs in them. Usually the animals have no significance beyond atmospheric or decorative value. For instance, in the twelfth chapter of *Rudin* (1856), when a carriage arrives at a country house, on the run-in it is 'accompanied by two enormous house-dogs, one yellow, the other grey, recently acquired. They were always squabbling, and were inseparable companions. An old mongrel then came out at the gate to meet them, opened his mouth as if he was going to bark but ended by yawning and turning back again with a friendly wag of his tail.'

Occasionally, a dog may carry a certain symbolic value. Katya, in *Fathers and Children*, a member of the younger generation, belongs in spirit to that of her elders, the traditionalists, and this can be seen not only from her music (Mozart) but also from Fifi, the aristocratic Borzoi bitch who is always at her side.

It may easily be imagined that the rural sketches are strong in this direction, and indeed, of the twenty-five essays, no fewer than twenty-three contain dog references; a dozen animals are named, from Astronom to Zhuchka. The detail varies from the merest mention to the most intimate portrait. Breeds range from mongrel to lordly hound; there are puppies and ageing patriarchs. Every canine posture and behavioural pattern is represented. To take a small example, in one sketch the narrator turns his eye on the occasion when dogs first meet each other, describing the whole wary and sniffy ritual as 'that Chinese ceremonial which is the special custom of their kind'.

In none of these references will you find any lapse of taste. Because of the writer's knowledge there is no exaggeration, distortion or undue sentiment. The dogs have had their pictures painted by a sympathetic master with his feet on the Russian ground. Turgenev is confident enough not to resist investing his dogs with human characteristics. His animals are credited with 'a constrained smile', 'a dignified growl', 'a noble self-importance', and so on. This is not exaggerated sympathy. Human-like behaviour is not imposed upon animals. We have seen these same characteristics in our own dogs; they invite depiction as imitators of men – it is what they do. Turgenev recognises a truth about the species: they are voluntary anthropomorphists, who would dress like us if they could.

Turgenev wrote the best dog story in Russian literature, 'Mumu', which soon became famous abroad. Alexander Herzen said that this work made him tremble with rage. In England Christina Rossetti described it as 'consummate, but so fearfully painful', and Thomas Carlyle said it was the most beautiful and touching thing he had ever read.

The story was written in 1852, when Turgenev was supposedly in prison for having published an unofficial obituary in praise of Nikolay Gogol, who had written a good deal of anti-establishment literature. The sentence was served in the comfortable house of a police chief. During the month-long ordeal he wrote down the story of Gerasim, a deaf-mute of six foot six, brought in from the countryside to work as a house-serf in Moscow at the whim of his mistress, who has seen him out in the fields. The giant is in for some setbacks, and these involve his acquisition of a dog, whom he calls Mumu because it is the only sound he can make.

This story draws on real life. There was such a mistress: Turgenev's mother, a fearsome domestic tyrant, permanently sorry for herself and down on everybody else; most of the other characters were real people too. The only departure from actual events comes at the end of the story, when, in Turgenev's version, Gerasim makes a brave gesture of defiance. Sad to say, the real-life prototype, Andrey, knuckled under, and never blamed the cruel mistress for his misfortune.

Even from this sketch it may be apparent that there is more to this story than the narrative. Without becoming a formulaic creation, Gerasim can be taken as a symbol of the oppressed Russian serf class that was not emancipated until 1861, and remained downtrodden long after that. It was unusual, and risky, for an author to point out so clearly the atrocities of the current social order, which placed absolute power in the hands of monsters who often abused it. For our purposes it is significant that the pathos in this story comes from the situation and misadventures of the dog after which it is named. No reader is going to get lost in socio-political undertones; this is a powerful dog story that has moved many to tears.

Mikhail Saltykov and Trezor

Something similar might be said of our second story, written in 1884 by Mikhail Saltykov (1826–89), a Russian satirist of the second half of the nineteenth century who used the pen name N. Shchedrin, often appended to give him a double-barrel. His works are local and topical, close to journalism, but through the best of them, especially the novel *The Golovlyov Family* (1876–80), he has won a place among the Russian giants. His misfortune was to be a man of talent born in an age of genius that was dominated by the masters of Russian literature. That his voice is heard at all is a tribute to his strength as a writer.

The story chosen for this selection is well-known in Russia, even though it is more portrait than narrative. We are taken through the life of Trezor, a low-born guard dog, who cheerfully endures deprivation because of his desire to serve his master by being good at his job. The happiest moment of his life comes when the master replaces his old chain with a spanking new one. Having no desire to escape, he can revel in the improved social status bestowed by his new form of constriction.

The story has a mildly sad ending, but its tone is so agreeable and amusing that the conclusion comes as a natural outcome, and can be read without pain. We are dealing with a sympathetic master, who nevertheless beats his badly fed dog whenever he thinks fit. None of this fazes Trezor; as he says, a dog has to be beaten or he might forget who is the boss, and then where would we be? This philosophical attitude, out of tune with his mistreatment, has the ring of truth to it. Dogs are known for closely adhering to monstrous owners – remember Bull's-Eye. At his entry into the story of *Oliver Twist* (Chapter 13) he is described as 'a white shaggy dog, with his face scratched and torn in twenty different places', who skulked into the room only to be kicked across it, and then left to coil himself up in a corner, quiet but contented, well-used to rough treatment. Even at the end of the novel, after first defying Sikes and running away when about to be drowned, the dog returns to be present when his master hangs himself, and he howls out his loss to the world. Bull's-Eye and Trezor are brothers in the blood, both of them true to their hard masters.

Humour is the chief characteristic of 'Good Old Trezor', and is at its most obvious in the language of the dog, whose speech shows a mixture of vulgar and educated Russian, as if the narrator has had trouble in translating from canine to human. He even uses Latin expressions, to the shame of our readers, who will need the supplied translations. His speech is at its best in a little dialogue with the master's children, after which we are let into Trezor's personal secret: his passion ('not all the time, but just now and then') for the snooty Kutka, another dog in the yard. One day the two of them manage to escape together, though Trezor pays for their lapse when they return.

This tale is to be enjoyed as a sadly amusing life story. Saltykov intended us to draw a parallel between the life of Trezor and that of the Russian underclass, satisfied with its awful condition, which left it deprived and exploited even after the Emancipation, and still delighted to exchange one stricture for another. But that is no more than the ghost of an idea, hidden behind the entertaining text, which is all that really matters.

Anton Chekhov and Chestnut Girl

Before becoming Russia's best-known playwright (almost adopted as one of our own in Britain), Anton Chekhov (1860–1904) first trained as a doctor, and then began his literary career as a writer of sketches and short stories. Initially, these were rather silly tales of airy amusement, but as time went by he put more into them before emerging as a skilled writer of prose. Ask any Russian, and he or she will tell you they admire this man's plays, but they consider his stories to be the best ever composed. 'Chestnut Girl' (1887) belongs to his early period, and it has no pretensions to greatness or profundity. The Russian title is *Kashtanka* – the word *kashtan*, chestnut, with a pretty feminine ending. It is the only name in this collection that has a meaning, and we have seen fit to give it an English rendering that brings this out. Similarly, we have anglicised the names of the other animals: a goose, a cat and a pig. (The latter, Miss Harriet, is known in other translations as Khavronya Ivanovna.)

Do not look for symbolic meanings here. This is a pleasant narrative with a strong storyline and a twist at the end. (Because of another neglectful master, it brings Chestnut Girl into line with Trezor and Bull's-Eye.) Poor girl, she gets lost one day, to be taken in by a circus clown, who looks after her well, and trains her up as part of his act. What happens during her début performance provides the surprise ending.

Humour is, once again, the driving force behind this story, most of it arising from the dog's confused impressions of us and our world. She has her own logic, and can never quite understand why other animals fail to see things and do things the way she does. The man who looks after her for most of the story is an endearing character, harassed by the need to eke out a living in the circus, from which he will be dropped if anything goes wrong. His chancy act depends on performances from creatures not normally biddable to the extent that he requires.

Through all of these stories the reader would be advised not to hurry, but rather to linger over the details, particularly of animal language. There are some exquisite moments when Chestnut has to learn how to live with a cat and a goose, different enough in temperament but even more so in language. The cat makes his meanings clear without saying much, but Chestnut cannot make head or tail of what the goose has to say. He talks in monologues with great passion, but there is something not quite right: 'Chestnut had thought that he talked so much because he was highly intelligent, but a little time went by and she lost all respect for him... she looked on him as a boring old windbag who stopped you sleeping.'

At one stage Chestnut believes that the goose is trying to 'demonstrate his trusting nature'. The idea of a goose with not only a trusting nature but also a desire to demonstrate it is worth dwelling on, and the text is full of amusing asides such as this. Joke after joke underlies the curious and mildly worrying storyline in a series of events experienced by unusual characters in unusual circumstances. Their unpredictable world is made even more surprising by a couple of dog's dreams that blur reality as far as it will go while still remaining recognisable.

This early story has remained a favourite with the reading public, not least because of its location in that strange territory between the known and the unknowable that links us with our not-so-dumb friends. The author was pleased with it. In 1891 he wrote a friend, 'Please arrange for a hundred copies to be sent to the administrative offices of the Society for the Protection of Animals.' What they did with them is not known.

Alexander Kuprin and Arthur

All of the stories discussed so far have been well written. One does not feel that a touch of skilful editing could make an improvement. But in the case of 'Arthur, the White Poodle', this is not so; we have taken some small liberties with his text. First, the name Arto, which is neither Russian nor English, has been extended to the more familiar Arthur. But there is more to it than that. The story needed shortening and tidying. It was issued in 1904 and later published in a collection of children's stories. The author was Alexander Kuprin (1870–1938), a novelist and short-story writer who found success with his first novel, *The Duel* (1905). His later years were spent abroad, mainly in Paris, though he returned home in 1937, and died in Leningrad the following year.

Allow children to read this story by all means. They will find great fun in it, especially when it culminates in an act of bravery by a young boy which will make them feel proud. If this sounds like the boyish adventures of Jack London (1876–1916), who wrote exciting dog or wolf stories that appealed to youngsters, so be it; Kuprin took London as a model. But adults should not shy away. This is good fun for all of us to read. It tells the tale of a small group of circus-type performers: an old man, his grandson, and their dog, Arthur, as they roam the beautiful Crimean Peninsula in summer, looking for work as entertainers in private holiday homes. In one of these, after a remarkable encounter with the posh family of a terribly spoilt child, they awake from sleep one day to find that their dog has been stolen, and the task will be to get him back. The characterisation is simple, but the changing situations and action are amusing and exciting. Arthur himself is a rewarding companion, and everyone will read this story with pleasure. If anything, Kuprin has been too ambitious in filling it out, as if extra length might give the story higher status. This does not work, and we have risked offence by shortening the account, especially towards the end. Nothing of importance has been omitted. Apologies are due to the shade of Alexander Kuprin, but surely he would have been proud to find himself in such good company as the other writers here included.

The final story is a splendid piece by the famous Ilf and Petrov – Ilya Fainzilberger (1897–1937) and Yevgeny Katayev (1903–42) – who wrote the two best satirical Russian novels of the twentieth century, *Twelve Chairs* (1928) and *The Golden Calf* (1931). They were also responsible for a string of stinging sketches ridiculing the excesses and dangers of life in Stalinist Russia. How they got away with such criticism for such a long time remains a mystery. It is astonishing to think that our story, 'Ich Bin from Head to Foot', was published in 1933, three years after the poet Mayakovsky shot himself partly because of the tightening grip of Stalinism on the artists of Soviet Russia. At that time anything that did not conform to Socialist Realism was called Formalism, a dangerous thing of which to be accused. The sad fates of many Russian creative artists in the 1930s remind us of the deadly seriousness of the issues involved.

And yet here we have a story in which the intrepid Captain Masuccio is brought over from Germany to perform a circus act with his talking dog, Brünhilde. Unfortunately, her modest repertoire smacks of Formalism. The actual term is not deployed, but 'bourgeois', 'middle-class', 'Humanism' and 'Art for Art's Sake' are, and the poor dog is accused of them all. What she is eventually required to learn and perform by way of a revised text will shock and amuse the reader. The machinations of the Circus Cultural Committee, ludicrous though they may seem, are accurately described, if contemporary reports are anything to go by. It is like the Political Correctness of our own age, only much worse and with murderous teeth. The real impact of this story emerges when you bear in mind the chasm that exists between the absurdity of the apparatchiki and the dire danger that their decisions could deliver to innocent victims in real life. One could have been shot in a cellar for Formalistic tendencies. Many were, though indeed many were shot in cellars for even less. By some miracle, the authors have drawn wonderful comedy from a perilous situation.

– Anthony Briggs, 2012

Five Russian Dog Stories

MUMU
by Ivan Turgenev

On one of Moscow's outlying streets, in a grey house with white columns, a mansard frontage and a crooked balcony, there once lived a landowning widow surrounded by a whole crowd of domestics. Her sons worked as civil servants in St Petersburg, her daughters were married off, and she rarely went out visiting. She was living out the last solitary years of her miserly and tiresome old age. Her day, joyless and foul, had passed long ago, and now the evening of her life was blacker than night.

Among her domestic staff one person stood out, a yard-keeper by the name of Gerasim, a man of six foot six, built like a giant, deaf and mute from birth. The mistress had brought him in from the country where he used to live on his own in a small shack away from his brothers; he was famous among the peasants for being first with the payment of his taxes. Endowed with phenomenal strength, he could do the work of four men, and anything he undertook was done well. It was a pleasure to watch him, whether he was out in the field, with his huge hands bearing down on the plough and cutting through the spongy bosom of the soil as if he was doing it all by himself without any help from his scraggy little horse; or when he laid about himself with his scythe to such devastating effect that, come St Peter's Day, you would swear he was stripping out a whole new birch wood, roots and all; or when he was threshing away with a seven-foot flail, flat-out, non-stop, and his solid-flexed shoulder muscles pounded up and down like pistons. His perpetual silence invested his unflagging work with a special gravity. He was a fine upstanding peasant, and but for his affliction any young girl would

3

willingly have had him for a husband. Anyway, Gerasim was brought into Moscow; they fitted him out with boots and a specially made summer smock and winter coat, handed him a shovel and broom, and set him up as yard-keeper.

At first, he didn't take to this new way of living at all. Man and boy he had been used to country life and working in the fields. Isolated by his affliction from other people's company he grew up strong and silent, like a tree in good soil. Resettled in the city, he hadn't the slightest idea what was going on – he was homesick and stunned, like a strapping young bullock hustled in from the meadow where he has been belly-deep in lush grass, and shoved into a railway wagon with smoke and sparks or gushing steam swirling around his well-fed body while he hurtles along – to God knows where – with a lot of banging and screeching.

Gerasim's duties in his new job seemed like a joke after all that hard work as a peasant; he got everything done in half an hour, and he would either come to a halt half-way across the yard, goggling at the people who went by as if he might learn from them how to solve the mystery of his new situation, or take himself off into a corner, where he would hurl away his broom or shovel, throw himself down on the ground and lie there without moving for hours on end, face-down, like a wild beast in captivity. But a man can get used to anything, and eventually Gerasim did get used to living in the city. There wasn't much for him to do; his work consisted of keeping the yard clean, fetching a barrel of water two or three times a day, bringing logs and chopping them to size for the kitchen or the main house, as well as keeping people out and guarding the place at night. And it must be said that he carried out his duties to the letter; you would never see as much as a sliver of wood in the yard, or any litter, and if the clapped-out old mare entrusted to him happened to get stuck in the mud while she was hauling a barrel in the rainy season, one shove with his shoulder would get it moving again, not just the barrel on the cart but the horse too. Once he had started chopping wood, the axe rang like glass in his hands, and splinters and sticks would fly about all over the place; and when it came to dealing with intruders, well, after that time when he caught a couple of thieves one night and banged their heads together with such a whack there was no point in handing them over to the police, everybody in the vicinity treated him with the greatest respect, and even when people walked past during the day, not criminals but unknown passers-by, they would take one look at the terrifying yard-man and wave him away, shouting across as if he could hear them. With the rest of the servants Gerasim was on not what you would call *friendly* terms – they were too scared of him – but they were close: he thought of them as 'our people'. They communicated with him by gesturing; he could understand them, and he did everything they told him to do, though he also knew his own rights, and none of them dared sit in his place at the table. In a word or two, Gerasim was a stern and serious character, a stickler for good order. Even the cockerels didn't dare have a scrap when he was around; they knew what was coming to them – the moment he saw them he would grab them by the feet, swing them round and round a dozen times and hurl them away in different directions. The mistress also kept geese in the yard, and everybody knows that your goose is a bird of quality who knows what he's about. Gerasim paid them proper respect; he looked after them, and fed them, rather fancying himself as a sedate-looking gander. He had been given a little room over the kitchen; he fitted it out himself the way he liked things, knocking up a bed of oak planks on four blocks – a bed for

5

Hercules! – you could have put a ton weight on it and it wouldn't bend. There was a strongbox underneath it, and in one corner stood a small table as solid as the bed, with a three-legged stool so chunky and squat that Gerasim would pick it up and clump it down with a smug grin on his face. His little room was locked with a padlock the size of a loaf, only it was black, and Gerasim always kept the key on his belt. He didn't like people coming up to see him.

A year went by like this, at the end of which Gerasim was involved in a little incident.

The old mistress whose yard he was keeping belonged to the old school in every way, which meant she had lots of servants: her household included not only laundry-maids and seamstresses, tailors and dressmakers, there was even a saddler who also served as a vet, though it was her own household doctor who took care of the staff, and finally there was a cobbler by the name of Kapiton Klimov, a terrible boozer. Klimov felt done down and undervalued; here he was, a man brought up in St Petersburg, the capital; Moscow was beneath him, he had no proper job, he was stuck in a backwater, and if he did take a drink, he drank only because of the grief he had to bear – he said it himself, slurring his speech and beating his breast. Then, one day, his name came up in a discussion between the mistress and her chief steward, Gavrilo, a man who, if his beady yellow eyes and his beaky nose were anything to go by, seemed to have been picked out by destiny itself to serve as a figure of authority. The mistress was sorry to hear about Kapiton's depravity – he had been picked up out on the streets only the day before.

'What about it, Gavrilo?' she broke out suddenly. 'Do you think we ought to get him married? It might bring him to his senses.'

'Well, why not, ma'am? It might work,' answered Gavrilo, 'Do him a power of good, ma'am.'

'Yes, but who would have him?'

'There is that, ma'am. Still, it's what you want that matters, ma'am. Anyway, he must be good for something. There are plenty worse.'

'Do you think he might fancy Tatyana?'

Gavrilo was about to raise an objection, but he bit his lip.

'Yes! Let him get married to Tatyana,' the mistress decided, taking a most agreeable pinch of snuff. 'Do you hear what I say?'

'Yes, ma'am,' said Gavrilo stiffly, and he withdrew.

The first thing Gavrilo did when he was back in his room (which was in one of the outbuildings, crammed with iron-bound boxes), was to send his wife away; he then sat down by the window with a lot on his mind. The arrangement suddenly proposed by the mistress had clearly put him on the spot. After some time he got to his feet and sent for Kapiton. Kapiton arrived... But, before we tell our readers how their conversation went, we think it will not be out of place to say a word or two about who she was, this Tatyana, the marriage prospect set up for Kapiton, and why the mistress' injunction had given the steward pause for thought.

Tatyana was one of the laundry-maids mentioned above (though she had had proper training in laundry-work so she was entrusted with the finest linen); a woman in her late twenties, small, thin and fair-haired, she had moles on her left cheek. Moles on the left cheek were considered a bad omen in good old Russia – the sign of an unhappy life. Tatyana had little to boast about. She had been badly treated since she was a young girl, having to do the work of two women and never being shown any affection; she was kept poorly dressed, and paid a pittance. She had no family to speak of, just an uncle who had once been in service but was now useless and left behind in the country, and one or two other uncles, common peasants, that was all. She had once been considered beautiful, but her good looks had soon slipped away. She was a submissive creature, you might say brow-beaten; she took no interest in herself and was mortally scared of everybody else. The only thing she thought about was how to get her work done in time; she never spoke, and she was reduced to a dithering wreck at the mere mention of the mistress's name, though the old lady scarcely knew her by sight.

When Gerasim had been brought in from the countryside, Tatyana had almost died of shock at the sight of his enormous figure; she gave him a wide berth, and she winced whenever she had to nip past him on her way from the house to the laundry. At first Gerasim ignored her, then he found it amusing when their paths crossed, then he started to look more closely, liking what he saw, and he ended up by not being able to take his eyes off her. He had fallen for her – it was either the meek look on her face that did it, or her timorous movements – heaven knows what. One day she was making her way across the yard, gingerly carrying her mistress' starched jacket on outstretched fingers when, suddenly, someone grabbed her by the elbow; she turned round and gave a yelp – there behind her stood Gerasim. With a stupid laugh and a tender grunt he was offering her a gingerbread cockerel with gold tinsel on its tail and wings. She wanted to refuse it, but he forced it on her, gave her a nod, walked away and then turned round to treat her to another very affectionate grunt. From that day on he never left her alone; wherever she went, he was there, coming towards her, smiling, grunting, waving his hands, magicking a ribbon from his smock and foisting it on her, and sweeping the ground where she walked. The poor girl hadn't the slightest idea how to respond or what to do. It wasn't long before the whole house knew what the dumb yard-man was up to; jokey remarks, silly sayings and caustic comments rained down on Tatyana. But there were some who held back from mocking Gerasim – he wasn't fond of jokes – and when he was around they left her alone. Like it or not, the girl was under his care. Like all deaf-mutes he was very sensitive, and he could tell immediately when people were laughing at him or her. One day over dinner the maid in charge of linen started getting at Tatyana, as people say, and soon got her into such a state that she didn't know where to look, until she was on the verge of tears from all the upset. Suddenly Gerasim was on his feet reaching out with his massive hand, bringing it down on the maid's head and glaring at her with such grim ferocity that she flopped down onto the table. Nobody said a word. Gerasim picked up his spoon and went on slurping his cabbage soup.

'See that? Dumb devil. He's a gremlin!' they were all saying under their breath, as the victim got up from the table and went off to the maids' room.

Then there was another occasion, when Gerasim, noticed that the same Kapiton of whom we have been speaking was getting too familiar with Tatyana. He beckoned him over with one finger, led him out into the coach-house, where he seized the end of a shaft that happened to be standing in a corner, and threatened him with it, gently but unmistakably. After that nobody dared try any fine words on Tatyana. And he got away with it all. True enough, when the linen-woman got to the maids' room she swooned away and acted up to such good effect that the mistress was informed about Gerasim's rough behaviour the same day; however, the capricious old woman did nothing but laugh, much to the consternation of the linen-woman, who was made to repeat what she had said about having her head shoved down by a heavy hand, and the next day the old lady sent Gerasim a one-rouble coin. She let him off on the grounds that he was such a good, strong guard. Gerasim was running scared of her, but he knew he was dependent on her kindness, and he was working himself up to requesting her permission to marry Tatyana. All he was waiting for was a new kaftan that the steward had promised him – he did want to be decently turned out when he appeared before the mistress – when suddenly it had occurred to this same mistress to marry Tatyana off to Kapiton.

The reader will now easily understand the reason behind Gavrilo's misgivings following his conversation with the mistress.

'The mistress,' he thought to himself as he sat by the window, 'is soft on Gerasim…' (Gavrilo was well aware of this, which is why he treated him so well), 'but when all's said and done he can't put any words together. Ought I to let the mistress know that Gerasim has his own designs on Tatyana? Not really, it's the right thing to do, isn't it? What kind of a husband would he make? Then again, the moment that gremlin (God forgive me) finds out that Tatyana is getting married to Kapiton, he'll wreck the place. That's for sure. There's no talking to him. You can't get round a devil like him (Lord have mercy on me, a sinner), really.'

The arrival of Kapiton broke the thread of Gavrilo's reflections. The feckless cobbler came in, put his hands behind his back, leant nonchalantly against the protruding angle of a wall near the door, placed his right foot across the front of his left foot, and tossed his head, as if to say, 'Here I am. What do you need me for?'

Gavrilo studied Kapiton, drumming his fingers on the window-jamb. All Kapiton did was to narrow his leaden eyes, without looking down; he then went so far as to give a little smile and run his hand through his whitening hair, which was left sticking out all over the place. Again the implication was, 'Yes, it's me. What do you think you're looking at?'

'Fine figure of a man,' said Gavrilo, pausing for a while. 'I don't think.'

All Kapiton did was to give a slight shrug of his skinny shoulders. 'You any better?' he thought to himself.

'Take a look at yourself. Just look,' said Gavrilo in a tone of reproach. 'Who are you supposed to look like?'

Kapiton looked down serenely at his torn coat and patched trousers, and scrutinised his worn-out shoes with particular care, especially the toe of the shoe that his right foot was so ostentatiously leaning against, then looked back at the steward.

'What about it?'

'What about it?' Gavrilo repeated. 'What do you mean, "What about it?" You look like the devil himself. (God forgive me.) That's who you look like!'

Kapiton blinked his beady eyes several times quickly.

'That's all right, Mr Gavrilo, names can't hurt me,' he thought to himself.

'I hear you've been drunk again,' said Gavrilo, launching forth. 'Drunk again... Well, say something.'

'I may have taken a drop of drink for medicinal purposes,' said Kapiton by way of objection.

'Medicinal purposes! They're too soft on you, that's what's wrong. And you've been in Petersburg studying. Fat lot of studying you did there. All you're good for is getting your daily bread for nothing.'

'As far as that's concerned, Mr Gavrilo, the Lord God alone is my judge – and nobody else. He alone knows what kind of man I am, living on this earth, and whether I'm getting my bread for nothing. And this drinking business, it's not my fault, it's one of my mates what done it, led me astray and got me all confused, then he went off, I mean, and I was…'

'And you were left there in the street, like an idiot. You're hopeless! Anyway, never mind that,' went on the steward, 'What I wanted to see you about was this. The mistress …' he paused, 'The mistress thinks it would be a good idea for you to get married. Do you hear that? She's got it into her head that being married would settle you down. Do you follow me?'

'Course I follows you, sir.'

'Well, that's how it is. In my opinion, what you need is a strong hand looking after you. Still, it's her business not mine… Well, what do you say?'

Kapiton grinned. 'Marriage is a fine thing for a man, Mr Gavrilo, and as far as I'm concerned – I'd be delighted to have the pleasure.'

'Very well,' said Gavrilo, with some reservations, though he thought to himself, 'Enough said. He knows how to string his words together.'

'There is one thing,' he added aloud, 'The girl they've picked out for you to marry isn't – quite right.'

'May I be asking who it is?'

'Tatyana.'

'Tatyana?' Kapiton goggled as he came away from the wall. 'What do you mean she isn't right, Mr Gavrilo? She's not a bad-looking girl, she knows how to work, she's nice and quiet… But listen, Mr Gavrilo, you knows yourself – that gremlin, that hobgoblin from the back of beyond, he's sweet on her…'

'All right, my friend, I know all about that,' said the steward, cutting across him with some irritation, 'but, er...'

'Oh please, Mr Gavrilo! He'll kill me, God knows he will. He'll squash me like a fly. He's got a hand like... sir, you knows what his hand's like... He's got a hand like Minin and Pozharsky's.[1] Besides, he's deaf... can't hear you when he's beating you up. Swinging his damn great fists like that – it's a nightmare. And you can't stop him. Why not? I'll tell you why not. You knows yourself, Mr Gavrilo, he's deaf, and more than that he's dead stupid, no more brains than the heel of my shoe. He's some sort of wild animal, a big stone statue, Mr Gavrilo, no – worse than that, he's like a great big tree. Why should I have to go through it with him? I know it doesn't make any difference, I've been worn down and I've got used to it, and I'm all greasy like a cheap old pot – but when all's said and done I'm still a man, I'm not really just a useless old piece of pottery.'

'I know. I know. Don't make it sound worse...'

'God in heaven!' the cobbler went on, warming to his theme, 'When will it ever end? When, for God's sake? I'm just a miserable wretch, down on my luck. I'm a no-hoper! What's fate ever done for me? Just think! When I was little I got beaten by a master who was German. In the première of me life I got bashed up by my brother, and now look, when I've reached a nice ripe age, look what things have come to...'

'Hey, that'll do, I've heard enough whingeing for today,' said Gavrilo, 'Going on and on like that, huh!'

'Like what, sir? I'm not scared of being beaten! I don't mind the master punishing me inside four walls as long as he says hello to me in public, then I belongs to yumankind. Now look who I'm going to have to...'

'Oh, get out of here,' said Gavrilo, impatiently cutting him short. Kapiton turned and went.

'Hey, what if he wasn't here?' the steward shouted after him. 'You wouldn't refuse, would you?'

'I would give my consent,' Kapiton shouted back, and he was gone, eloquence not having deserted him even in extreme circumstances.

The steward walked up and down the room a couple of times.

'Right. Let's send for Tatyana,' he said at last.

A few moments later Tatyana came in almost without being heard, and stopped in the doorway.

'What do you want me for, sir?' she said in a low voice.

The steward looked at her closely.

'Well then,' he said, 'Our little Tanya, how would you like to get married? The mistress has found you a bridegroom.'

'Yes, sir. Who've I got as a bridegroom?' she said with no confidence.

'Kapiton. The cobbler.'

'Yes, sir.'

'He's a bit flighty, I'll give you that. But that's where the mistress is depending on you.'

'Yes, sir.'

'There's just one thing. That, er, deaf chap, Gerasim. He seems to be rather sweet on you. How did you manage to charm a great big bear like that? Anyway, he's likely to kill you, big bear like that.'

'Oh yes, he will, sir. He'll kill me all right.'

'Kill you, will he? Well, we'll see about that. How can you say he'll kill you? Do you think he has any right to kill you? Just think about it.'

'I don't know, sir. Whether he does or he doesn't.'

'Funny girl. By the way, you haven't, er, *promised* him anything, have you?'

'Beg pardon, sir?'

The steward did not reply. He was thinking, 'Can't get anything out of you, can I?'

'Very well,' he said. 'We'll have another little chat later on. Off you go now, little Tanya. I can see you're a nice quiet girl.'

Tatyana turned to go, brushed against the door-frame, and walked out.

'Oh well, maybe tomorrow the mistress will have forgotten all about this marriage,' thought the steward. 'Why have I got so worked up about it? That trouble-maker – we'll tie him up and maybe hand him over to the police... Ustinya!' he roared across to his wife. 'Put the samovar on the table, my treasure!'

Almost all day long Tatyana stayed inside the laundry. At first she burst into tears, but then she wiped them away and went back to keeping busy with her work.

Kapiton sat in the pub until last thing at night with some sort of gloomy-looking friend, telling him in great detail how he had lived with one master in Petersburg who would have been fine and dandy if he hadn't been too finicky about things, and he was a great tippler and when it came to the fair sex he wasn't at all choosy... His gloomy friend never stopped nodding, but when Kapiton finally announced that he had a good reason to lay hands on himself tomorrow morning, the same gloomy friend suddenly noticed it was time for bed. Their parting was gruff and silent.

In the event, the steward's hopes were not to be realised. The mistress was so taken with the idea of Kapiton's marriage that she stayed up that night talking about nothing else to a lady companion who was kept on simply to be there and help out with insomnia – like a cab-driver on nights, she slept during the day. When Gavrilo reported in after morning tea her first question was, 'And how is our wedding coming along?' Naturally enough, he said things couldn't be better; Kapiton would be coming in that very day to pay his respects. The mistress had something wrong with her, so she wasn't spending a long time over business matters.

The steward went back to his room and called a meeting. This question needed a lot of discussion. Tatyana was not going back on her word, of course, but Kapiton informed the world at large that he only had one head, not two, not three... Gerasim kept glancing at them all with a quick scowl, and he wouldn't budge from the maids' building; it seemed to be dawning on him that something bad was being hatched up against him. Those present (including an old footman nicknamed Uncle Tail, to whom they all turned for advice even though the only thing they ever heard him say was, 'There we have it then. Yes, yes, yes...') began by taking one precaution: for safety's sake Kapiton was locked up in the little storeroom with the water-filtering machinery. Then they got down to some serious thinking. It would be easy enough to use force, of course, but God forbid it should come to that, with all the noise upsetting the mistress – that would be catastrophic. What could they do? They thought and thought, and finally came up with an idea. It had often been noticed that Gerasim had no time for people who got drunk. As he sat at the gate he would turn away in disgust whenever a man who had been at the bottle came staggering past with the peak of his cap over one ear. It was decided that Tatyana must be taught to look as if she had been drinking and walk past Gerasim, rocking and reeling. For a long time the poor girl refused to do it, but they talked her round, and in any case she came to see that there was no other way of getting rid of her admirer. She went ahead and did it. Kapiton was let out of the storeroom – after all, he was involved in this. Gerasim was sitting at the gate on a low round stone scratching the ground with his shovel. From round every corner, from behind every blind, eyes were on him.

The trick paid off better than anyone could have expected. When he caught sight of Tatyana, at first he started nodding towards her and making his soft mooing noises, then he looked more closely, dropped his shovel, got to his feet and walked over to her, bringing his face close up to hers… She was so scared she swayed more than ever and shut her eyes… He took her by the hand, rushed her straight across the yard, went into the room where the meeting was being held and shoved her straight at Kapiton. Tatyana nearly fainted. Gerasim stood there looking at her, gave a twisted grin, and stomped off with a wave of his hand back to his room.

He didn't come out for twenty-four hours. Antipka, the postboy, told them later on that when he looked in through a crack he could see Gerasim sitting on his bed with one hand against his cheek, now and then making soft, rhythmic mooing sounds to himself; he was singing, which meant rocking backwards and forwards with his eyes closed and shaking his head about like a driver or a barge-hauler when they let go with their sad songs and the long, drawn-out melodies. Antipka found it too scary, and he came away from the crack. But when Gerasim came out of his little room the next day, there was no noticeable change in him. Maybe he looked a mite gloomier, and he completely ignored Kapiton and Tatyana.

That evening they went together to see the mistress, with geese under their arms by way of a present, and one week later they were married. On the day of the wedding Gerasim didn't change his routine one iota, though he did come back from the river without any water, having somehow smashed his barrel on the way, and at night-time in the stables he scrubbed and rubbed his horse so vigorously that it swayed like a blade of grass in the wind, rocking from one leg to another under his iron fists.

All of this had been happening in springtime. Another year went by, which saw Kapiton become a slave to the bottle, and being a completely useless individual he was dispatched by cart-train to a remote village, along with his wife. On the day of their departure he put a brave face on it at first, insisting that, wherever he was sent, even to a place where women 'wash the shirts beneath the sky, but hang the washboard up to dry', he wouldn't let them grind him down. But then his spirits fell, and he started moaning about being sent away to mix with ignorant people, and finally he was reduced to such a state that he couldn't put his cap on straight; it took a compassionate soul to pull it round over his forehead, straighten the peak and tap it down. When everything was ready, and the peasants were holding the reins while they waited for the words, 'Off we go, and God go with us!' Gerasim came out of his room, went up to Tatyana and gave her a souvenir; it was a red cotton scarf he had bought for her a year or so ago. Tatyana, who until this moment had borne all the setbacks of her life with perfect indifference, broke down at last, burst into tears, and before getting up onto the cart exchanged three kisses with Gerasim like a true Christian. He intended to see her off as far as the toll-gate, and at first he walked along with the cart, but suddenly at the Crimean Ford he stopped, gave a dismissive wave of the hand and walked off along the riverbank.

It happened as evening was coming on. He was walking quietly along, staring at the water. Suddenly he thought he saw something floundering in the mud near the bank. Bending down, he saw a little black-and-white puppy struggling like mad and unable get out of the water. It was flapping about, slipping all over the place and shivering all along its sopping, thin little body. Gerasim took one look at the miserable little dog, pulled it out with one hand, shoved it under his coat and set off home, striding out. He came into his little room, put the dog he had just saved down on the bed, covered him with a heavy coat, nipped across to the stable to get some straw and then round to the kitchen for a little bowl of milk. Delicately pulling back the coat, he spread out the straw and put the milk down on the bed. The poor little thing was barely three weeks old, its eyes had only just opened, and one of them actually looked a bit bigger than the other one. She didn't yet know how to drink from a bowl; all she did was shiver and screw her eyes up tight. (She had turned out to be a bitch.) Gerasim picked her up by the neck, gently between finger and thumb, and bent her little snout down to the milk. Suddenly the little dog started slurping greedily, snorting, shivering and choking as she did so. Gerasim watched and watched, and then burst out with a sudden laugh. All night long he fussed over her, putting her to bed and wiping her dry, and when at last he dozed off he was lying next to her, and his sleep was restful and happy.

No mother could have looked after her baby better than Gerasim looked after his new charge. At first she was a feeble, sickly and ugly little thing, but as time went by she pulled herself together and straightened out so that when eight months or so had gone by, thanks to the untiring efforts of her saviour, she had grown into a nice spaniel with long ears, a fluffy tail shaped like a trumpet, and big eyes full of feeling. She had become passionately devoted to Gerasim, sticking to his heels, and walking behind him everywhere with her tail gently wagging. He gave her a name; mutes are aware that their mooing noises attract attention, and he called her Mumu. All the household servants fell in love with her, and they called her by her pet-name, Mumúnya. She was very intelligent, she wanted to be petted by everybody, but Gerasim was the only one she loved. And Gerasim loved her to distraction; he didn't like other people stroking her. Heaven knows whether he was afraid for her or just jealous. She woke him up in the morning by tugging at the hem of his coat, and she would bring up the old horse who pulled the water barrels, leading him by his reins (they were good friends); she would also go down to the river with him wearing an expression of great self-importance; she guarded his brooms and spades, and she wouldn't let anyone near his room. He cut a hole in his door especially for her, and she seemed to think that Gerasim's room was the one place where she was in complete control, which meant that when she came in she jumped straight onto the bed, looking pleased with herself. At night she never slept, nor did she set off barking for no good reason like a stupid mongrel sitting back with its snout in the air, narrowing its eyes and barking from having nothing better to do, barking at the stars or nothing in particular, usually three times in succession – no! Mumu's soft voice was never put to use without good reason – if, for instance, an outsider came near to the fence, or there was a suspicious noise or a sound of something rustling. In a nutshell, she was an excellent guard dog. Actually, there was another dog in the yard besides her, an old yellow-and-brown hound called Volchok, but he was never let off his chain, not even at night, and he himself, feeble as he was, never wanted to be set free – he just lay there curled up in his kennel, now and again producing a hoarse kind of bark, nearly inaudible, which he cut short straight away as if he knew how completely useless it was. Mumu never went into the big house, and when Gerasim was carrying firewood into the rooms, she would always stay outside and stand impatiently by the steps waiting for him to come back, with her ears pricked and her head moving right and then sharply left whenever she heard the slightest noise from inside.

In this way another year went by. Gerasim went about his yard-keeping duties, and he was very happy with the way things had worked out, until one day an unexpected event suddenly occurred.

What happened was this: one fine day in the summertime, the mistress was walking round the drawing room accompanied by her lady companions, the usual hangers-on. She was in a good mood, laughing and joking, and the ladies were playing along, also laughing and joking, but without much enthusiasm. The household didn't enjoy it when the mistress had one of her happy hours because, firstly, she instantly demanded a totally sympathetic response, and she would fly into a rage if she saw anybody with a face that wasn't beaming with pleasure, and, secondly, these outbursts of hers never lasted long and they were usually followed by a mood of nasty bitterness. That morning she had got up with a lucky feeling. At cards she had been dealt four knaves, a sign that her wishes would come true (she always liked a bit of fortune-telling in the morning), and she had particularly enjoyed her tea, for which the maid got a compliment (words), and a tip (money). She had a sweet smile on her wrinkled lips as she strolled round the room, ending up at the window. There was a small flower garden just under the window and there, under a little rosebush right in the middle, lay Mumu, busily gnawing at a bone. The mistress spotted her.

'Good heavens!' she suddenly exclaimed, 'Whose dog is that?'

The lady to whom the mistress had turned panicked, the poor little creature, filled with the kind of miserable anxiety that usually overtakes a person subject to another's will when it is not quite clear what kind of response is required to an exclamation from the master.

'I… er, I'm n-n-not too sure,' she mumbled. 'I think it might belong to the dumb man.'

'Good heavens!' said the mistress, interrupting her. 'Isn't she a sweet little dog? Have her brought in. How long has he had her? How can it be that I haven't seen her before? Do have her brought in.'

The lady rushed out into the hall.

'You there!' she called out, 'Go and get Mumu, now. She's in the flower-bed.'

'Oh, she's called Mumu,' said the mistress. 'What a nice name.'

'Yes, very nice, madam!' put in the lady companion. 'Do get a move on, Stepan!'

Stepan, a burly youth serving as a footman, rushed out headlong into the garden and made a grab for Mumu, but she slipped through his fingers, lifted her tail and ran flat-out back to Gerasim, who was busy bashing a barrel and scraping it clean outside the kitchen; it was rolling through his hands like a toy drum. Stepan rushed after her, and got a bit of a hold on her close to her master's legs, but the nippy little dog was jumping and wriggling, determined not to fall into somebody else's hands. Gerasim watched this scuffle with amusement. Eventually Stepan got up with some irritation and lost no time in signalling to him by gesture that the mistress wanted his dog taken inside. Gerasim was somewhat taken aback, but he called Mumu, lifted her up and handed her over to Stepan. Stepan took her into the drawing room and put her down on the parquet floor. The mistress put on a simpering voice and called her over. Mumu was scared – she had never in her life been inside rooms as grand as these – and she dived for the door, only to be shoved back in by the obliging Stepan. She ended up hugging the wall and shivering.

'Mumu. Mumu, come here, come to the mistress,' said the grand lady. 'Come on, you silly little thing. Don't be afraid.'

But Mumu was looking around gloomily, and didn't move a muscle.

'Get her something to eat,' said the mistress. 'What a silly thing she is! Not coming to the mistress. What can she be afraid of?'

'She's not quite used to you yet,' said one of the companions in a timid, soppy voice.

Stepan fetched a saucer of milk and put it down in front of Mumu, but Mumu wouldn't even give it a sniff; she was still shivering and looking around.

'Now, what's this all about?' said the mistress, walking over to her. She bent down, wanting to stroke her, but Mumu jerked her head away, and snarled. The mistress snatched her hand away.

There was a moment's silence. Mumu gave a feeble whine, as if she wanted to complain or apologise. The mistress walked away scowling. The dog's sudden movement had frightened her.

'Oh dear!' exclaimed all the lady companions at once. 'I hope she hasn't bitten you. God forbid!' (Mumu had never bitten anybody in her life.) 'Oh dear! Oh dear!'

'Get her out of here,' said the mistress in a changed tone of voice. 'Nasty little thing! What a savage!'

And, turning slowly away, the mistress made her way through to her boudoir. The companions looked nervously at each other and followed on quickly, but she stopped, gave them a cold glance, and said, 'What's all this about? I haven't called you.' And off she went.

The companion ladies waved desperately at Stepan; he picked Mumu up and threw her outside in short order, right at the feet of Gerasim – and within half-an-hour a profound silence reigned over the whole house. The old mistress sat on her sofa with a face darker than thunder.

To think what stupid little things can upset some people!

All afternoon the mistress was out of spirits; she spoke to nobody, didn't play at cards, and went on to have a bad night. She got hold of the idea that the eau de cologne she had been given wasn't the same as the eau de cologne she usually received, and that her pillow had a soapy smell, so the linen-woman had to come in and sniff all the bedclothes. All in all, she was deeply upset and she 'flew off the handle' rather a lot. Next morning she had Gavrilo summoned an hour earlier than usual.

'Just tell me this,' she began the moment he had crossed her threshold in some trepidation. 'Whose dog was that barking all night long in our yard? I never got a wink of sleep.'

'Dog, madam? What dog would that be, madam? Ah, perhaps you mean the dumb man's dog, madam.' He spoke in a less than confident tone.

'I don't know whether it's his dog or somebody else's. All I know is it wouldn't let me sleep. In any case, I'm surprised we have such an abundance of dogs. Tell me something. Do we or do we not have a yard dog?'

'Er, yes, madam. We do, madam. Volchok, madam.'

'Well, why do we need any more? Why should we need

another dog? It's just looking for trouble. There's no discipline in this house – that's what's wrong. And why does the dumb man need a dog? Who gave him permission to keep dogs in my yard? I went to the window yesterday, and there it was in the flower-garden with some ghastly thing it had brought in, chewing at it – just where I've had roses planted.'

The mistress paused.

'I want it out of here – today… Do you hear what I say?'

'Yes, madam.'

'I mean today. Off you go. I'll hear your report later on.'

Gavrilo walked out.

As he passed through the drawing room the steward transferred a little bell from one table to another, to keep things tidy, and quietly cleared his beaky nose in the ballroom before going through into the hall. In the hall there was Stepan fast asleep on a chest, looking like a slain warrior in a battle scene, with his bare legs thrust out from under his coat, which was being used as a blanket. The steward shook him awake, and gave him some instructions in a low voice, to which Stepan responded with something that was half-yawn, half-guffaw. The steward then went away, and Stepan hopped down from his chest, pulled on his kaftan and boots, and went outside by the front steps. Barely five minutes had passed when along came Gerasim carrying a big load of firewood on his back, accompanied by the inseparable Mumu. (The mistress required her bedroom and boudoir to be heated even in summertime.) Gerasim turned side-on to the door, shoved it open with his shoulder and flopped forward into the house carrying his load. As usual Mumu sat outside waiting for him to come back. Stepan, seizing his chance, flung himself down on her like a hawk on a chicken, pressed her chest down to the ground, snatched her up under one arm, and rushed out of the yard without bothering to put his cap on; outside, he hailed the first cab that came along, and it took him down to Hunter's Row. Here he soon found a purchaser, giving him a half-rouble discount on condition that he kept her tied up for at least a week; then he set off back, but he got out of his cab well short of home, and walked right round the outside of the yard and down a backstreet, where he got in by climbing the fence because he was scared of running into Gerasim if he went in through the front gate.

As it happened, he needn't have worried. Gerasim wasn't there. The moment he left the house he missed his Mumu, and, since he couldn't remember her ever having given up waiting for him, he rushed about all over the place looking for her, calling her as best he could. Dashing back to his room, then to the hayloft, and outside onto the street – here, there and everywhere. She had gone! He turned to the servants, asking after her with the wildest despairing gestures, pointing one-foot-high and shaping her with his hands. Some of them, who simply didn't know where Mumu had gone, just shook their heads; others knew about it and they chuckled up their sleeves by way of an answer. And as for the steward, he took on an air of great importance, and went round shouting at the coachmen. At this point Gerasim ran out of the yard and away.

It was getting dark when he came back. If his tired look, unsteady walk and dusty clothing were anything to go by, it seemed as if he had been chasing half-way around Moscow. He stopped by the windows of the big house, looked at the front steps, where half-a-dozen servants had gathered, turned away and gave one last call of 'Mumu!' But there was no answer from Mumu, and he walked away. They all watched him as he went, but no one smiled and not a word was spoken. The next morning the post-boy Antipka, ever curious, told them in the kitchen that the deaf-mute had been moaning and groaning all night long.

The next day Gerasim didn't put in an appearance, which meant that the water had to be fetched by a coachman called Potap, and coachman Potap wasn't too pleased about this. The mistress asked Gavrilo whether her instructions had been carried out. Gavrilo said yes, they had.

On the following morning Gerasim left his room and came out to work. He dropped in for his dinner, ate it and went off again without giving anybody the time of day. His face, lifeless enough anyway (as with all deaf-and-dumb people), seemed to have turned to stone. After dinner he left the yard again, but not for long; he soon came back and headed for the hayloft. Night came on, moonlit and clear. Sighing deeply as he tossed and turned, Gerasim lay there until all of a sudden he seemed to feel something pulling at the hem of his coat; he shivered all over, but instead of looking up he screwed his eyes up tight – then came another tug, stronger than before. He sat up, and there in front of him was Mumu, circling with a bit of torn-off rope round her neck. A long, long moan of delight came from his unspeaking breast; he grabbed at Mumu, holding her close in his arms, and in a second she had licked him all over his nose, eyes, moustache and beard.

He stood there for a moment, thinking things over, before climbing down carefully from the hayloft. Then, with a cautious look around to make sure he wasn't being watched, he found his way safely back to his room. Gerasim had already worked out that his dog had not gone missing all by herself. No, she must have been spirited away to please the mistress – the other servants had signalled to him that she had snapped at her – and he knew what he had to do. The first thing was to feed Mumu, so he gave her some bread. Then he gave her a cuddle and put her to bed, and spent the whole night worrying about how best to hide her. Eventually he worked it out: he would leave her in his room all day and come to visit her only now and then, and he would take her out at night. He stuffed up the hole in the door with an old coat, and at first light he was out in the yard as if nothing had happened, making sure (with the subtlety of an innocent!) that his former misery still showed on his face.

Poor deaf man that he was, it never occurred to Gerasim that Mumu would give herself away by yelping. Everybody in the house, in fact, soon knew that the deaf man's dog had come back, and was locked up in his room, though out of pity for him and his dog, and partly perhaps because they were scared of him, no one let on that they knew his secret. The steward was the only one who scratched his head and gave a hopeless wave of his hand, saying, 'Good luck to him. Maybe the mistress won't get to know.'

The dumb man, though, had never worked as hard as he did that day. He washed the yard and scraped it clean, weeding every last corner; he pulled out all the posts in the fence round the flower-garden with brute force, checked them for strength, and banged them back in again; he – well, he fussed about and took so much trouble over everything that even the mistress noticed how keen he was. During the day Gerasim popped in a couple of times on the quiet to see his little prisoner, and when night came on he went to bed with her in his room rather than in the hayloft; it was past one o'clock when he took her out for a walk in the fresh air. After quite a long turn about the yard he was just about to take her in again when suddenly there was a shuffling sound from the back street on the other side of the fence. Mumu pricked up her ears and growled, walking over to the fence, where she first sniffed around and then launched into a loud, ear-splitting bark. Some drunk had seen fit to settle down there for the night.

At that moment the mistress was just nodding off after a long bout of 'the nerves': those fits that always came upon her when she had overeaten at the dinner table. The sudden barking woke her up; her heart leapt and fell.

'Girls, girls!' she moaned. 'Girls!' Terrified maids rushed into her bedroom. 'Oh dear, I'm dying!' she managed to say, with a weary spread of her hands. 'It's that dog again. Oh dear, get me the doctor! They're trying to kill me. That dog. It's that dog again! Oh dear!' and she threw her head back in a gesture of fainting. The doctor was sent for, or rather the household medical helper, Khariton. This medicine man – whose expertise comprised nothing more than an ability to go around in soft-soled shoes, to take a pulse with a delicate touch, to sleep away fourteen hours of the twenty-four, and to spend the rest of his time regaling the mistress with laurel drops – this quack came running in, wafted her with some singed feathers, and was standing by when the mistress opened her eyes, with a glass of the sacred drops on a little silver tray. The mistress took them, and lost no time in raising her tearful voice again to complain about the dog, Gavrilo, and her hard lot in life – what a poor old woman she was, abandoned by everybody, nobody had any time for her, they all wanted her dead. And all this time the luckless Mumu went on barking while Gerasim made vain attempts to call her back from the fence.

'Listen… There it is again…' the mistress murmured, rolling her eyes upwards. The doctor whispered to a maid, who rushed into the hall and shook Stepan awake; he shot off to rouse Gavrilo, and a bad-tempered Gavrilo ordered everybody up.

Gerasim turned round and caught sight of lights flashing against shadows in the house; sensing disaster in his heart, he snatched up Mumu and stuffed her under his arm, ran back to his room and locked himself in. Gavrilo came running up, panting for all he was worth, and told them all to stay where they were and keep watch till morning; he himself raced off to the maids' quarters, where he used an intermediary, Lyubov Lyubimovna, the senior lady companion with whom he raided the tea and doctored the accounts, to inform the mistress that unfortunately somehow the dog had found its way back, but tomorrow it would no longer be alive, and would she graciously refrain from being too angry with them, and remain calm. The mistress would probably not have remained at all calm but for the medicine man who, in his hurry, had given her not twelve drops but no fewer than forty; the strength of the laurel water took effect, and within a quarter of an hour the mistress was fast asleep and breathing easily. Meanwhile Gerasim lay on his bed white-faced and holding Mumu's mouth tight shut.

The next morning the mistress awoke rather late. Gavrilo had been waiting for her to come round before ordering them to close in once and for all on Gerasim's sanctuary, and he himself was getting ready to withstand a violent storm. But no storm came.

Lying in bed, the mistress sent for the eldest lady companion.

'Lyubov,' she began in a soft and feeble voice (she sometimes liked to play the part of a downtrodden, suffering orphan-girl, and, needless to say, when she did so all the household servants felt distinctly uneasy). 'Lyubov, you can see what a state I'm in. Would you mind having a word with Gavrilo, my dear? Ask him whether he considers some stupid little dog more important than his mistress' peace of mind, even her life? I wouldn't like to think so,' she added, with a look of deep feeling. 'Go now, darling. Please. Go and see Gavrilo.'

Lyubov set off for Gavrilo's room. It is not known what transpired between them, but soon afterwards a whole crowd of servants could be seen making their way across the yard, heading for Gerasim's little room. Gavrilo strode out in front, clutching his cap even though there wasn't any wind, and the footmen and the cooks came too. Uncle Tail was watching through the window, telling them what to do by waving his arms about, and at the back some rough lads, half of them outsiders, were jumping about and showing off. A guard sat on the narrow stairs leading up to Gerasim's little room; by the door there were two more, holding sticks. They all ended up spread out all over the staircase, occupying it from bottom to top. Gavrilo went up to the door, banged on it with his fist, and called out, 'Open up!'

There came a stifled yap, but no reply.

'I'm telling you to open up!' he repeated.

'Gavrilo,' said Stepan from down below. 'Don't forget, he's deaf. He won't hear you.'

They all laughed at this.

'What shall we do then?' Gavrilo responded from the top.

'Look, there's a kind of opening there,' said Stepan. 'Shove your stick through and shake it about.'

Gavrilo bent down.

'Yes, it's a hole, but he's stuffed it up with a coat or something.'

'Why not shove it in?'

Another muffled yap came through the door.

'Listen. She wants you to know she's there,' came a voice from the crowd, and they all laughed again.

Gavrilo scratched behind his ear.

'No, my friend,' he said at last. 'You come and shove it through, if that's what you want.'

'All right. Let me come past.'

Stepan made his way to the top of the stairs, took one of the sticks, pushed the coat through to the inside, banged about with the stick and said, 'Come on! Come on out!' He was still banging away when the door was flung wide open, and all the servants barrelled down the stairs, with Gavrilo in the lead. Uncle Tail closed his window.

'Hey, you up there!' Gavrilo shouted from down in the yard. 'I'm telling you. Watch what you're doing!'

Gerasim stood there in the doorway without moving. A crowd had gathered at the foot of the stairs. Gerasim looked down on these tiny people dressed like Germans, with his hands gently resting on his hips; in his red peasant's shirt he looked like a giant towering above them. Gavrilo stepped forward.

'Look here, my friend,' he said. 'Don't you play around with me.' And he set about explaining in sign language: the mistress wants your dog, no two ways about it, and you'd better hand her over or you'll live to regret it.

Gerasim looked at him, pointed at Mumu and then at his own neck, pretending to tighten a noose round it, and then he looked quizzically at the steward.

'Yes, that's it,' said Gavrilo, nodding his head. 'Definitely.'

Gerasim looked down, then suddenly he shook himself and pointed at Mumu again – she was standing at his side innocently wagging her tail and waggling her ears as if puzzled. He mimed the strangling again round his own neck, and then thumped himself on the chest meaningfully – a clear indication that it was his job to destroy Mumu.

'I can't trust you,' said Gavrilo with a dismissive wave.

Gerasim glanced at him, gave a twisted smile, thumped himself on the chest again, and banged the door shut.

They all looked at each other in silence.

'What was all that about?' began Gavrilo. 'Has he locked himself in?'

'Let him be, Mr Gavrilo,' said Stepan. 'He'll do it, if he promised. That's what he's like. He'll definitely do anything he's promised to do. He's not like us, you know. What's right is right. Oh yes.'

'Yes,' came from all sides, and heads were nodding. 'That's how it is. Oh yes.'

Uncle Tail opened his window, and said yes too.

'Oh, all right. We'll see what happens,' said Gavrilo, 'But keep guarding him. Hey you, Yeroshka,' he added, turning to a rather pale-faced man dressed in a cotton Cossack coat who passed himself off as a gardener. 'Not too busy, are you? Get yourself a stick and sit here. Anything happens, you come and let me know. At the double!'

Yeroshka got himself a stick and sat down on the bottom step. The crowd dispersed, apart from one or two nosey-parkers and some young lads, and Gavrilo went back to his place, where he sent Lyubov to let the mistress know that her wishes had been carried out to the letter, and that he had sent the post-boy to get the policeman just in case. The mistress tied a knot in her handkerchief, sprinkled it with eau de cologne, took a sniff at it, dabbing herself on the temples, had a good drink of tea and went back to sleep, still lulled by the laurel drops.

An hour after all this bother the door to the little room was flung open, and there stood Gerasim. He was wearing his best long-coat; he had Mumu on a string lead. Yeroshka edged away and let him through. Gerasim walked to the gate. The young lads and all the people in the yard watched him go without saying a word. He didn't even turn round, and he didn't put his cap on until he was out on the street. Gavrilo sent Yeroshka after him as an observer. From a long way off Yeroshka saw him go into the tavern with his dog, and he settled, waiting for him to come out again.

Gerasim was well-known in the tavern, and they could read his signals. He ordered some meat and cabbage soup for himself, with both hands resting on the table. Mumu stood by his chair, watching him calmly with her sharp little eyes. Her coat was glossy; she had obviously just been combed. They brought Gerasim's soup. He crumbled some of the bread into the soup, cut the meat up into little pieces and put the plate down on the floor. Mumu began to eat in her usual fastidious way, with her little muzzle scarcely touching the food. Gerasim watched her for some time; suddenly two tears rolled down from his eyes, one falling onto the little dog's flat brow, the other into the soup. He covered his face with one hand. Mumu ate her way through half a plateful, and then walked away licking her chops. Gerasim got up, paid for the soup and walked out, accompanied by a rather puzzled look from the waiter. Yeroshka saw Gerasim come out, nipped round a corner to let him go past, and then followed on behind.

Gerasim was walking steadily down the street, keeping Mumu on the lead. When he got to the corner he stopped and seemed to think things over, but then suddenly he set off at a fast pace, heading straight for the Crimean Ford. Along the way he slipped into the yard of a house where an extension was being built and came out carrying two building blocks under his arm. At the ford he walked along the riverbank until he came to a place where two rowing-boats with shipped oars were moored, tied to pegs. He had noticed these previously, and now jumped into one with Mumu. An old chap hobbled out of a hut in one corner of a kitchen garden, and shouted at him. But Gerasim just nodded and set off rowing, upstream, so powerfully that in no time he had covered nearly two hundred yards. The old man stood there for quite a while, scratching his back, first with his left hand and then with his right, and then hobbled back into his hut.

Meanwhile, Gerasim was rowing steadily on. Before long Moscow had been left behind. A bit further on, meadows, gardens, fields and woodland lay along the riverbank, and peasant shacks began to appear. There was a breath of country air. Gerasim shipped the oars with a thump, bent down close to Mumu, who was sitting in front of him on the dry seat – the bottom of the boat being awash – and stayed there in one position without moving, with his big strong hands crossed over her back, while a wave started to carry the boat little by little back towards the city.

Eventually Gerasim sat up straight, and acted quickly with a painful bitterness written on his face, tying string round the bricks that he had brought with him, making a noose to put round Mumu's neck, lifting her out over the river, and taking one last look at her... She looked at him in complete trust and without fear, gently wagging her little tail. He looked away, screwed up his eyes and unclenched his hands... Gerasim heard nothing, neither the little squeal that Mumu gave as she fell, nor the big splash; for him the noisiest day was more silent and soundless than the softest night could be for us, and when he opened his eyes wide the wavelets still seemed to be chasing each other downstream, still lapping against the sides of the boat – the only difference was way behind, where wide circles were rippling out speedily towards the riverbank.

Yeroshka had watched Gerasim row out of sight, and now he set off immediately back home to report all that he had seen.

'Oh yes,' said Stepan, 'He was going to drown her all right. You could be sure of that. As long as he had promised...'

No one saw Gerasim again that day. He didn't have his lunch with them. Evening came on, and everyone turned up for supper, except him.

'Funny chap, that Gerasim!' a fat laundrywoman said in a squeaky voice. 'Fancy getting all worked up like that over a dog... I don't know!'

'He's been back here, Gerasim.' Stepan spoke out suddenly, spooning up his gruel.

'You what? When was he here?'

'Oh, a couple of hours ago. Oh yes, it was him all right. I ran into him by the gate. He was on his way out, leaving the yard. I, er, wanted to ask how things were with the dog, but he didn't seem in the mood somehow. Actually he banged into me. I'm sure he was only shoving me away, telling me to keep clear, but he caught me one round the back of me neck, and I'm tellin' you it didn't half hurt!' Stepan couldn't help smiling as he hunched his shoulders and rubbed the back of his neck. 'Oh yes,' he added. 'He has a delicate touch, he does. You can't deny that.'

They all laughed at Stepan, and when supper was over everyone went off to bed.

Meanwhile, at that very time, a gigantic figure was striding out purposefully along the road to T–, carrying a sack over his shoulders and a big stick. He wasn't stopping. It was Gerasim. He was hurrying along without a backward glance, hurrying back home, back to the countryside where he had been born. After drowning poor Mumu he had run back to his room, thrown a few things together and bundled them up in an old horse-cloth; then he was off. He had taken careful note of the way they were going when they had brought him into Moscow; the village from which the mistress had taken him was a good bit less than twenty miles off the high road. He walked along in a spirit of unstoppable boldness, a mixture of despondency and jubilant determination. As he walked his chest swelled; his eager eyes looked steadily ahead. He was flying along as if his old mother was waiting for him at home, as if she was calling him back after a long spell of wandering in foreign parts among foreign people…

The summer night had just drawn in, mild and warm; in one direction, where the sun had gone down, the skyline still shone white, with a light touch of pink from the last flush of the declining day, and in the opposite direction a grey-blue twilight was coming up. That was where night was coming from. Quails screamed in hundreds on every side; corncrakes called across to each other one by one. Gerasim couldn't hear them any more than he could hear the gentle night-time rustling in the trees that his strong legs were taking him past, but he could appreciate the familiar smell of ripening rye wafting across from the dark fields, and feel the wind – a wind that came from home – blowing gently into his face and playing with his hair and his beard, and he could see the road shining white ahead of him, the road home, running as straight as an arrow, and the infinite number of stars lighting his way, and he strode out like a lion, so manfully and in such good heart that by the time the rising sun cast its first moist-pink rays on the strong young figure now nicely into his stride, he had put twenty miles between him and Moscow.

It took him two days to get home and back to his small hut – which came as a shock to the soldier's wife who had been billeted there. After mouthing a prayer before the icons he set off straight away to see the headman of the village. The headman reacted at first with some surprise, but, with hay-making just under way and Gerasim known as an excellent workman, they shoved a scythe into his hands; off he went to do some haymaking just as he had done before, and his mowing left the other peasants open-mouthed at the sight of huge amounts piling up from his swinging and raking.

Meanwhile, back in Moscow Gerasim was missed the day after he absconded. They went into his little room, ransacked it and went to tell Gavrilo. He came along, took a look at things, and decided with a shrug that either the deaf-mute had run away or he had drowned himself along with his silly dog. They informed the police and told the mistress. The mistress was furious; she burst into tears, told them to find him, whatever it took, made it clear that she had never ordered the dog to be put down, and gave Gavrilo such an earful that he went about for a whole day shaking his head and saying, 'Oh my…' until Uncle Tail brought him to his senses by saying, 'All your *what?*' Eventually news came through from the village that Gerasim was back home. The mistress calmed down a little. At first she ordered him to be brought back to Moscow immediately, but then she announced that she had no need whatsoever for such an ungrateful person. In the event, she died soon afterwards, and her heirs had no time to bother with Gerasim. They freed the rest of the mistress' serfs in exchange for payment of an annual tax.

And Gerasim still lives there, a lonely figure in his little shack, as strong and fit as ever. As before, he does the work of four men, and, also as before, he values his dignity and keeps things in good order. But his neighbours have noticed that since his return he has kept away from the company of women, not even looking at them, and he won't keep a dog.

'Oh well,' say the peasants. 'He's a lucky man doin' without women. And dogs? Why would he need a dog? Wild horses and strong men wouldn't bring a thief on to his bit of land.' That's what the world says about the dumb man and his colossal strength.

1852

SLY DOG

Last spring I left the house and set off for a stroll,
To watch the time unroll
   And let the springtime air bring comfort to the soul.

   A Dog came by, fawning in every feature,
   Apparently a very friendly creature.

   Not knowing yet his business or intent,
   I went to stroke his head, and bent.
   He stopped his fawning all too quickly,
      And as I offered him a hand – he went and bit me,
   And then he ran away.

   So, have no truck with toadies. Keep them all at bay,
   Reader! All toadies are of that same ilk, the blighters!

They turn and bite us.

A.A. Rzhevsky, 1761

GOOD OLD TREZOR
by Mikhail Saltykov

Old Trezor was the guard dog at a granary belonging to
Vorotilov, a second-guild Moscow merchant, and he guarded
his master's property with an unsleeping eye. He never left
the vicinity of his kennel; he hadn't ever had a proper look
down Knacker's Row, where the store was located. From
morning till night he did nothing but leap about at the end of
his chain, barking furiously. *Caveant consules!*[2]

And he was a wise old bird, never barking at his own
people, only at outsiders. If the coachman came by looking
to pinch a few oats, old Trezor would give him a wag, thinking
to himself, 'He'll not be taking a lot.' But the moment a
stranger walked past the yard, minding his own business, and
old Trezor heard him, it would be, 'Help! Thieves! Help!
Help!'

Merchant Vorotilov would see Trezor working away like
this, and he would say, 'That dog's worth his weight in gold!'
And if he happened to walk past the kennel on his way to the
granary he would invariably say, 'Give old Trezor some slops!'
And old Trezor would be beside himself with delight.

'My pleasure, sir! Arf, Arf! You can rest easy, sir. Arf! Arf!
Arf!'

One day a funny thing happened. No less a figure than the
police chief deigned to set foot in the yard, and old Trezor
had a good go at him too. He raised hell, and they all came
running out – master, mistress and children. They thought
they were being robbed, but when they looked – oops, it's
an important visitor!

'Do come in, your Worship! Make yourself at home! Shush,
Trezorka. What are you on about, you stupid animal? Can't

41

you see who it is? Eh? Have a drop of vodka, your Worship. A quick snack?'

'Thank you. Splendid dog you have there, Nikanor! Very loyal!'

'Yes, he's a good 'un! A good lad. Not many men as savvy as he is.'

'Knows what property is, and nowadays... well it's very nice to see that!'

And then he turned to Trezor and went on speaking.

'Bark, my friend, you carry on barking! Nowadays, you take a man – if he wants to give a good impression of himself, he's got to bark like a dog!'

Vorotilov had tempted Trezor three times before entrusting all his property to him. He had dressed up as a thief (the outfit suiting him down to the ground!), waited for a night when it was a bit darker than usual, and then gone to the barn to steal some stuff. On this first occasion he took a crust of bread along with him with every intention of tempting the dog, but old Trezor gave it one sniff and promptly sank his teeth into the back of his leg. On the second occasion Vorotilov threw the dog a whole length of sausage, and said, 'Take, Trezor, take!' but Trezor took a piece out of his coat-tail. The third time, he took him a smeary banknote, expecting the dog to react to money, but old Trezor wasn't having it; he made such a racket that dogs ran in from all over the district only to stand there wondering why on earth a house dog was barking at his master.

At this, Vorotilov called the staff together, and in front of them all he said to Trezor, 'All my worldly goods, Trezor, I am entrusting to you. My wife, my children, my things – you guard them all for me! Bring some slops out for old Trezor!'

Whether or not old Trezor understood this praise from his master, or whether he did it by himself because that's what a dog does, his bark sounded like something thundering out of an empty barrel, and from that point on he was the perfect dog. He could have one eye fast asleep and the other one watching for anybody slipping in under the gate. When he got tired of galloping about he would lie down to rest, but his chain would go on clinking – 'Watch it, I'm still here!'

And if they forgot to feed him he was delighted. A dog shouldn't be fed every day, it's too much; give him a week of that, and he won't be a real dog any more! If they kicked him about he took that as a useful warning: stop beating a dog, and see what happens – he'll forget who's boss.

'Us dogs, we needs the right treatment,' was his way of thinking. 'Beat us when we do, beat us when we don't. Good lesson. It's the only way we'll ever get to be real dogs!'

This is to say he was a dog of principle, and he set his sights so high that the other dogs would just stare and stare, and slink off with their tails between their legs – 'Can't compete with that!'

On top of that old Trezor was a lover of children, though he didn't give in to them. The master's children would come up and say, 'Come on, Trezorka. Walkies!'

'I can't come.'

'You're too scared.'

'I'm not scared. I don't have the right.'

'Come on, you stupid thing! We'll sneak out. Nobody will see!'

'What about my conscience?' And old Trezor would put his tail between his legs and skulk in his kennel, to avoid temptation.

Times without number thieves would put their heads together: 'Let's show him a picture-book – *Scenes of the Moscow River.*' Even that wouldn't tempt him.

'Don't need no scenes,' he would say. 'I was born in this yard, and this is where I shall lay down me old bones. Don't need no more scenes. Get lost. Go and sin somewhere else.'

Old Trezor did have one weakness: he was hopelessly in love with Kutka, though not all the time – just now and then.

Kutka lived in the same yard, and she was a good dog herself, but she had no principles. She would start barking and then just stop. Anyway, she wasn't chained up, and she spent most of her time down by the master's kitchen, knocking about with the master's children. In her time she had guzzled down lots of sweet stuff, and she never shared any of it with Trezor. He didn't hold this against her; she was a lady, and she needed her sweet stuff. But when Kutka's heart began to speak to her she would whine softly outside the kitchen door and scratch at it with her paw. The moment he heard that quiet little yelping, old Trezor knew what to do: he set up such a racket, and it was so much his thing, you might say, that the master would get the message and come rushing out himself to protect his property. Trezor was let off his chain, and his place was taken by the yardman, Nikita. And Kutka and Trezor, blissfully excited, would run off together down to the city gate.

On these days Vorotilov easily lost his rag, and when old Trezor came back home the morning after his day out, his master took his whip and thrashed him without mercy. And Trezor obviously knew he had done wrong because he didn't come swanning up like an official who has done a nice piece of work – no, with his tail between his legs he would cringe and crawl up to his master's feet, and instead of yelling from pain as the blows fell he would cry out, '*Mea culpa! Mea maxima culpa!*'[3] He was clever enough to understand that, in doing what he did, his master was ignoring the extenuating circumstances; nevertheless, looking at it logically, he couldn't avoid the conclusion that if he didn't get beaten under those circumstances he definitely wouldn't be a real dog any more.

But if there was one really endearing feature about old Trezor it was his complete lack of ambition. There's no way of telling whether he had the slightest inkling of what holidays meant or that when their saint's days came round business-men were in the habit of handing out gifts to their good old servants. Come *his* day (Nikanor's) or *her* day (Anfisa's), it was always an ordinary weekday for Trezor, jumping about on his chain!

'Stop that racket, you vile thing!' Anfisa would yell at him. 'Don't you know what day it is?'

'Don't bother. Let him bark,' Nikanor would come back, jokily. 'He's talking to the angels. Keep barking, old chap. You keep on barking.'

The only time he showed a vestige of ambition was when the town cowman had a bell hung round the neck of that cow of theirs, Rokhla, who butted everything in sight. To be honest, he did feel jealous when she walked round the yard dingalinging.

'It's all right for you, but what have you done to deserve this?' he said to Rokhla, full of spite. 'All you do is let them take half a bucketful of milk out of you every day, but when you look at it, what kind of work is that? You get your milk free. It's independent of you. When they feed you well, you give lots of milk; when they don't, you don't. You never stir a hoof in the master's service, and look what rewards you get! And me – I'm at it day and night, all on my own, *motu proprio*.[4] Not

45

enough to eat, not enough sleep. Bark meself hoarse from all the comings and goings. You'd have thought they might chuck me a rattle and say, "Here you are, old Trezor. Just so you know all your good work does get noticed!"'

'What about your chain?' Rokhla had the wit to ask.

'My chain?'

Now he understood. Up till now he had thought that a chain was just a chain, but it turns out that a chain is something like a masonic emblem, which meant that he had had his reward right from the start; he had had it even at a time when he hadn't done anything to earn it. And now there was only one thing he could long for: a time when his rusty old chain (which he had broken once) was taken away and he was bought a new one, good and strong. It was as if Vorotilov had overheard his modestly ambitious hankering: when Trezor's name-day came round, he brought him a brand-new chain of wonderful workmanship, and clipped it onto Trezor's collar to surprise him.

'Get barking, Trezor. You get barking.'

And he sang out with the kind of serenely dulcet barking that comes only from dogs who make no distinction between their own canine contentment and the security of the barn to which the hand of the master has assigned them.

All things considered, old Trezor had a great life, but, naturally enough, from time to time there were one or two setbacks. In the world of dogs, as in the human world, sycophancy, foul play and envy have a function which is not theirs by right. On the odd occasion old Trezor had felt pangs of envy, but he had a strong sense of duty and he was quite without fear. Not that this had anything to do with having a high opinion of himself. No, he would have been the first to lose face and give way to any new arrival who could claim top-dog status by being invincible. In fact, he would often have alarming thoughts about who might step into his place when old age or death put an end to his inexhaustibility... But alas! In the entire pack of degenerate, barked-out dog denizens of Knacker's Row, in all honesty there wasn't one he could point to and say, 'There's my successor!' So, if ever a plot was got up to run down old Trezor in Vorotilov's eyes, stopping at nothing, it would end up with only one (unwanted) result: a demonstration of the universal diminution of canine talent.

On a couple of occasions envious guard dogs, singly or in little packs, would come together in Vorotilov's yard, and mount a challenging stand-off aimed at Trezor. An unimaginable canine cacophony built up steadily, which dismayed all the servants, though it puzzled the master when he heard it, because he knew full well that the time was approaching when old Trezor was going to need a bit of assistance. There were one or two decent voices that stood out in this choral frenzy, but there wasn't a trace of one scary enough to turn your stomach. The odd dog would show signs of outstanding quality, but the barking was always overdone or underperformed. While these bouts were under way old Trezor usually kept his own counsel at first, as if to let the contestants have their fair go, but before they got to the end, when he could take no more of the generalised moaning, every last note of which gave an impression of strained artificiality, he would come in with his own way of barking, a model of free-flowing sobriety. This barking dispelled any doubts. When she heard it, the cook would dash out from her kitchen and throw boiling water over the conspirators. Then she would bring some slops out for old Trezor.

Nevertheless, merchant Vorotilov had been right in his claim that nothing under the moon lasts for ever. One morning his deputy walked past the kennel area on his way to the granary, and caught Trezor asleep. This had never happened before. Whether or not he did sleep – he probably did – nobody knew; anyway, no one had ever caught him in the act of sleeping. Naturally the deputy lost no time in reporting this extraordinary occurrence to the master.

Merchant Vorotilov came out in person to see old Trezor and watched him wagging his tail like a penitent as if trying to say, 'I've no idea how I could have done such a sinful thing.' In a voice devoid of anger and full of sympathy he said,

'So that's it, old chap – time for the kitchen? Getting on, getting feeble? All right, you can go in the kitchen and work there just as well.'

For the time being, though, a decision was taken to do no more than find a helper for old Trezor. It was no easy task, but after going to endless trouble they did manage to discover down near the Kaluga Gate a certain dog by the name of Arapka, who had built up a fairly solid reputation.

I shall not describe how Arapka was the first to knuckle under, bowing to old Trezor without question; how they became pals; how old Trezor was eventually transferred once and for all into the kitchen; nor how, in spite of this, he kept running out to see Arapka and taught him the tricks of the trade as a proper merchant's watchdog, out of the goodness of his own heart. I will just say one thing: not the free time, nor the many treats, nor the closeness of Kutka, nothing, could make old Trezor forget the inspirational times he had enjoyed sitting at the end of his chain and shivering from the cold through the long winter nights.

Time passed, though, and old Trezor got older and older. A growth came up on his neck, forcing his head down to the ground, so badly that he could hardly get up. His eyes became virtually sightless, his ears flopped down limply, his coat was all matted and coming out in handfuls, his appetite was gone, and a permanent feeling of cold kept the poor dog pressed up against the stove.

'Say what you will, Mr Nikanor, but old Trezor is getting all scabby,' the cook announced one day to Vorotilov.

On this occasion, Vorotilov didn't say a word. But the cook was not going to be placated, and a week later she spoke again.

'What if the children go and catch something from old Trezor? He's scabby all over.'

Even on this occasion Vorotilov kept silent. Then, two days later, the cook ran in seething with rage and announced that she wasn't staying on a minute longer unless Trezor was removed from her kitchen. And since the cook was a dab hand at sucking-pig on buckwheat, a dish which Vorotilov loved to distraction, old Trezor's fate was sealed.

'Not the kind of thing I trained him up for,' said merchant Vorotilov with deep feeling. 'Yes, people are right when they talk about a dog having a dog's death. Trezor has got to be drowned!'

So Trezor was taken outside. All the servants flocked out to watch the death throes of the good old dog; even the master's children appeared at the windows. Arapka was there too, and when he saw his old teacher he gave him a welcoming wag. Because of his advanced age old Trezor could hardly put one foot in front of another, and he didn't seem to take anything in, but when they were getting down by the gate his strength failed him, and he had to be dragged over the ground by the scruff of his neck.

What happened next has not gone down in history, but old Trezor never came back.

And before long Arapka had driven any vestige of Trezor's image out of Vorotilov's heart.

1884

BEGGAR AND DOG

A Dog stood in his master's spacious yard.
In came an old man with his scrip, all dirty.

The Dog barked at him, keeping guard.

'I'm a poor fellow. Please have mercy!'
Whispered the old man, shaking, full of dread.
'I have not eaten. I shall die from hunger!'

'That's why I bark like thunder!'
The Dog said. 'Am I here *to see you fed*?'

Appearances can so deceive the righteous.
Beasts can be kind, and gentle folk can bite us.

I.I. Dmitriyev, 1804

CHESTNUT GIRL
by Anton Chekhov

1
Bad Behaviour

A young chestnut-coloured dog, a dachshund-mongrel cross with a foxy muzzle, was charging up and down the pavement, glancing around anxiously in every direction. She would stop now and then to lift up one frozen front paw followed by the other, whimpering as she tried to work out how she could have got herself lost.

She had a clear recollection of how she had spent the day, and how she had eventually landed up on this unfamiliar bit of pavement.

The day had begun with her master, Mr Luke the carpenter, putting his cap on, sticking a wooden object wrapped in a red cloth under his arm, and calling to her, 'Come on, Chestnut Girl, we're off!'

When she heard her name the dachshund-mongrel cross came out from under the bench where she slept on wood-shavings and ran after her master. Luke's customers lived an awfully long way away, so, before completing his visits to them one by one on his round, the carpenter had to slip into a pub several times to fortify himself. Chestnut Girl could remember behaving very badly on the round. She was so delighted to be taken out for a walk that she kept frisking about, barking at the horse-trams, running off into side-yards and chasing after other dogs. Every so often, when the carpenter lost sight of her, he would stop and call her name angrily. Once, with impatience written all over his face, he had even grabbed her by a foxy ear, yanked it and told her off in no uncertain terms.

'Drop... dead... you... damn... little... pest!'

After visiting all the customers, Luke had slipped in to see his sister, staying to have a drink and a snack. From her place he went on to a bookbinder of his acquaintance, and from the bookbinder he went into a pub, and from the pub he went to see one of his old mates, and so on. To put it plainly, by the time Chestnut Girl found herself on unfamiliar pavement evening was coming on, and the carpenter was three sheets to the wind. He was waving his arms about, sighing deeply and mumbling to himself, 'Born in sin from me mother's womb. Oh, my sins! What sins! Here we be walkin' down the street lookin' up at the lights, but when we dies we'm set to burn in hellfire...'

Either that, or he would go all sentimental, calling Chestnut Girl back and talking to her.

'Here you are, Chestnut, not much more than an insect. 'Longside a man, you'm like a joiner 'longside a cabinet-maker...'

While he was chatting to her like this they suddenly heard a blast of music. Chestnut Girl looked round and saw a regiment of soldiers marching down the street straight towards her. She couldn't abide music – always too much for her nerves – so she galloped off, howling. To her amazement the carpenter, far from looking terrified, and yelping and barking, gave a big grin, came to attention, and saluted with all fingers raised to his cap. Seeing that her master was making no protest, Chestnut Girl howled even louder, lost her head and dashed across the street to the opposite pavement.

When she came to her senses the music had stopped, and the regiment had gone. She crossed back to the spot where she had left her master, but alas! He was no longer there. She ran forward, ran back and crossed the street again, but the carpenter seemed to have vanished into thin air… Chestnut Girl set to, sniffing the pavement in the hope of tracking her master by the scent of his footprints, but just before that some blighter had walked past wearing new rubber overshoes, and now all the subtle smells were mingled in with the sharp stink of rubber so she couldn't tell what was what.

Chestnut Girl rushed up and down without finding her master, and by now it was getting dark. Street lamps came on down both sides of the road, and lights lit up the windows of the houses. Snow fell in thick, fluffy flakes, leaving a white covering on the road surface, the horses' backs and the cabbies' caps, and as the air got darker the objects stood out all the whiter. Chestnut had her view blocked and her body jostled by the legs of unknown customers walking hither and yon in an endless stream. (Chestnut divided humanity into two very unequal sections, masters and customers. There was one essential difference between the two: the first lot had the right to beat her, but she had the right to snap at the heels of the others.) The customers were in a hurry, and they were all ignoring her.

When it was quite dark Chestnut Girl was full of fear and despair. She huddled up in a doorway, crying bitterly. She was exhausted from walking about all day with Mr Luke, her ears and paws were frozen, and on top of that she was desperately hungry. She had only had a couple of things to chew all day: at the bookbinder's she had been given a bit of paste to eat, and in one of the pubs she had found a small piece of sausage-skin by the bar – and that was it. If she had been a man, she would probably have been thinking, 'No, this kind of life is impossible. Time to shoot myself!'

2
A Mysterious Stranger

But Chestnut Girl wasn't thinking about anything, she was only crying. When the soft fluffy snow had completely covered her back and head, and she had fallen into a deep snooze from sheer exhaustion, suddenly the door behind her squeaked, creaked and banged against her side. She jumped up. A man in the customer category walked out through the newly opened door. When Chestnut Girl yelped and got under his feet he could hardly ignore her. He bent down and spoke to her.

'Where've you come from, little doggie? Did I hurt you? Oh, you poor little thing! Now, don't get cross with me… I'm sorry.'

Chestnut looked at the stranger through the snowflakes over her eyelashes, and she saw before her a short, tubby little man with a chubby, clean-shaven face, wearing a top-hat and an unbuttoned fur coat.

'What's all this whining about?' he went on, brushing the snow off her back with one finger. 'Where's your master? You've got lost, haven't you? Poor little doggie! What shall we do, then?'

Cottoning on to the note of warmth and affection in the stranger's voice, Chestnut licked his hand and treated him to an even more pitiful whine.

'Good dog. You are a funny little thing,' said the stranger. 'Just like a fox. All right, there's only one thing to do – you're coming with me. You might even come in useful.' And he made a funny little whistling noise. He smacked his lips, and gave Chestnut a hand-signal that could only mean, 'Come with me!', which she did.

Within half-an-hour she was sitting on the floor in a large, bright room, with her head cocked to one side, a picture of tenderness and curiosity as she watched the stranger eating his breakfast at the table. As he ate he threw bits of food down to her. First he gave her some bread and a piece of green cheese-rind, then a bit of meat, half a pasty and some chicken bones, and she was so ravenous that she gobbled the lot down without tasting anything. And the more she ate, the hungrier she felt.

'Your masters haven't been feeding you very well!' said the stranger, noticing the furious greed with which she gulped down the un-chewed morsels. 'You aren't half thin – all skin and bone.'

Chestnut ate a lot, but without stuffing herself; she just became a bit woozy from eating. After her meal she sprawled in the middle of the room, stretching her legs out and letting her whole body luxuriate in the feeling of happy relaxation. She gave a wag. While her new master flopped into an arm-chair and smoked a cigar she carried on wagging and started to weigh things up: where was she better off – here with the stranger or back with the carpenter? With the stranger the whole set-up was mean and unsightly; apart from the armchairs, a sofa, one lamp and a few bits of carpet he owned nothing, and his room looked empty, whereas the carpenter's place was crammed with all sorts of things: he had a table, a workbench, a pile of wood-shavings, planes, chisels, saws, a little bird in a cage, and a wooden tub for washing things… The stranger's room had no smell, whereas the carpenter's was always filled with a haze and the magnificent smell of glue, varnish and shavings. But the stranger had one big advantage: he gave her lots to eat, and, to do him justice, when Chestnut sat at his table and looked at him pleadingly, he had never once hit her, he didn't stamp his feet, and he never shouted, 'Get gone, you blasted bitch!'

When he had finished his cigar the new master went outside and soon came back holding a little mat.

'Over here, dog!' he said, putting the mat down in a corner. 'This is your bed. Go to sleep here!'

Then he put the lamp out and left the room. Chestnut Girl sprawled across the mattress and closed her eyes. From the street came the sound of barking, and she wanted to respond, but suddenly she was overcome with a feeling of sadness. She remembered Mr Luke, his son Fedya, and her cosy corner under the bench... She remembered the long winter evenings when the carpenter was doing a bit of planing or reading aloud from his newspaper, and Fedya would play with her. He would drag her out from under the bench by her back legs and put her through such a routine of tricks and games that her vision turned green and she ached in every joint. He would make her walk about on her hind legs, use her like a bell, which meant pulling her tail until she yelped and barked, and give her tobacco to sniff. One trick was particularly painful: Fedya would tie a bit of meat onto a length of thread and give it to Chestnut, and when she had swallowed it he would yank it back out of her stomach, roaring with laughter. And the clearer her memories became, the louder and more pathetic was her whimpering

But it wasn't long before weariness and warmth won out over sadness... She began to doze off. In her imagination she saw dogs running around, and there racing past her was the shaggy old poodle she had seen that day out on the street, the one with blank white eyes and hairy tufts round his nose. Then came Fedya, armed with a chisel, chasing after the poodle, and suddenly he was covered in shaggy hair, barking away happily, and he fetched up close to Chestnut Girl. Chestnut Girl and he sniffed noses nicely, and ran out onto the street.

3
Another Acquaintance, and a Very Nice One Too

When Chestnut Girl woke up it was light outside, and the noise that came in from the street was the kind you only hear in the afternoon. There wasn't a soul in the room. Chestnut stretched, yawned and set off, gloomy and irritated, to inspect the room. She sniffed the corners and the furniture, and glanced into the hall without registering anything of interest. In addition to the door leading into the hall there was another one. After a moment's reflection Chestnut scratched at it with both paws, opened it up and walked through into the next room. There, on a bed, covered with a flannelette blanket and fast asleep, lay the customer whom she recognised as yesterday's stranger.

'Grrrr…' In mid-growl she remembered yesterday's meal, wagged her tail and started sniffing.

She sniffed the stranger's clothes and boots, and discovered that they had a strong horsey smell. Another door led out of the bedroom, but it was also closed. Chestnut scratched at that door, shoved against it with her chest, and immediately scented something unusual, something suspicious. Anticipating an unpleasant encounter, still growling and on the *qui vive*, Chestnut walked into the dingily decorated box-room, and then recoiled in alarm. She had seen something unexpected and horrible. With its neck and head pressed down to the floor, spreading its wings and hissing, the thing walked straight towards her – a greylag goose. Just to one side of it, lying on a mat, was a white cat, which, when it caught sight of Chestnut Girl, jumped up, arched its back, raised its tail, stood its fur on end, and also began to hiss. The dog was scared – this was no joke – but, not wanting to show any fear, she gave a loud bark and rushed at the cat. The cat arched his back even higher, hissed again, and smacked Chestnut Girl on the head with his paw. Chestnut leapt back, and shrank down on her four paws, extending her snout towards the cat and barking and yelping at him at the top of her voice. Meanwhile the goose had gone round to the rear to give her a good pecking down her back. Chestnut leapt up and ran at the goose.

'What's all this?' came a loud, angry voice, followed into the room by the stranger, in his dressing-gown and sporting a cigar in his mouth. 'What's the meaning of this? Back to your places!'

He went to the cat, tapped him on his arched back and said, 'Master Freddy, what *is* the meaning of this? Fighting? You old scallywag! Lie down!'

Then he turned to the goose, and shouted at him. 'Master Johnny, back in your place!'

The cat lay down obediently on his little mat, and closed his eyes. If the expression on his snout and whiskers was anything to go by, he was annoyed with himself for having lost his rag and got into a fight. Chestnut Girl whimpered, as the offended party, but the goose stuck out his neck and spoke rapidly, passionately and with careful enunciation, saying something quite incomprehensible.

'That's quite enough,' said the master with a yawn. 'We've all got to live in peace and friendship.' He stroked Chestnut and went on, 'And you, rusty, you've nothing to be frightened of… These are nice people. They won't hurt you. Hang on

59

a minute. What are we going to call you? You can't go about without a name, old pal.'

The stranger thought for a while, and said, 'That's it. You're going to be "Auntie". Have you got that? *Auntie!*'

And then, after repeating the word 'Auntie' several times, he walked out. Chestnut sat down to take stock of things. The cat sat on his mat, showing no movement, pretending to be asleep. The goose, stomping up and down on the spot and still sticking its neck out, had gone on annunciating at full tilt and with great passion. He seemed to be a highly intelligent goose; after every lengthy outburst he would pull back with an air of bemusement and look thoroughly pleased with what he had been saying.

Chestnut was listening and responding with her 'Grrr ...', but then she set off to have a good sniff in all the corners. In one of them she came across a little wooden tray with some soaking peas on it and some sopping rye-bread crusts. She sampled the peas – not very nice – then the bread, which she tucked in to. The goose was not at all put out by watching a strange dog lay into his food; quite the reverse, he spoke out with more passion than ever, and, to demonstrate his trusting nature, he came over to the tray and helped himself to a few peas.

4
Wonders to Behold!

After a while the stranger came back in carrying a funny object that looked rather like a gateway-frame based on the Greek letter *pi* (Π). There was a pistol tied to the crossbar of this wooden *pi* mock-up, and a big bell hanging down from it;

a string hung down from the tongue of the bell and the trigger of the pistol. The stranger put his *pi* down in the middle of the room, spent quite a while untying and re-tying things, and then looked at the goose and said, 'Master Johnny, you're on!'

The goose came over to him, and stood there with an air of expectation.

'Right,' said the stranger, 'Let's start at the top. First thing, you've got to *bow* and *curtsey*. Do it!'

Master Johnny stuck his neck out, nodded right, left and centre, and slapped his foot on the floor.

'Good boy! Well done! Now… *die*!'

The goose lay on his back and stuck his feet in the air. The stranger ran through a few more simple tricks like these, and then suddenly clutched the back of his head, and shouted out with a horrified look on his face, 'Fire! Fire! Help! Help!'

Master Johnny ran across, took the string with his beak and rang the bell.

The stranger looked well satisfied. He stroked the goose's neck, and said, 'Well done, Master Johnny! Now, I want you to imagine you are a jeweller dealing in gold and diamonds. Then imagine that you arrive at your shop and surprise some thieves. What would you do in those circumstances?'

The goose took the other string in his beak and pulled it, the immediate result of which was a deafening bang from the pistol. Chestnut really took to this sound; when she heard the bang she was so ecstatic that she ran round and round the letter *pi*, barking.

'Auntie! Back in your place!' the stranger yelled at her. 'And keep quiet!'

Master Johnny's work was not over just because he had fired a gun. For a good hour after that the stranger had him running around on a lead while he cracked his whip, and the goose had to jump a hurdle or leap through a hoop, or 'show his hind legs', which meant sitting back on his tail and waving his feet in the air. Chestnut Girl couldn't take her eyes off Master Johnny; she whimpered with delight, and once or twice she went rushing round after him, barking the place down. When he had worn them both out, the goose and himself, the stranger mopped his brow and called out.

'Marya, call Miss Harriet!'

A moment later there was a grunting sound. Chestnut growled, putting on a brave face, but, as a precaution, she edged up a bit closer to the stranger. The door opened, and an old woman glanced in, muttered something and ushered in an extremely ugly black pig. Completely ignoring Chestnut's growls, the pig cocked its snout in the air and grunted with delight. It seemed overjoyed to see them all again, its master, the cat and Master Johnny. When it walked over to the cat and gave him a gentle prod under his belly with its snout before getting into some kind of conversation with the goose, you could sense a great fund of good will in its movements, its voice and its quivering tail. Chestnut Girl immediately realised there was no point in growling and barking at characters such as these.

The stranger removed his *pi* construction, and called out, 'Master Freddy, *please*!'

The cat rose, slowly stretching, and walked over to the pig reluctantly, as if he was doing someone a favour.

'Good. Let's begin with the "Egyptian Pyramid",' the master began.

He spent some time explaining things, and then he gave the word of command.

'One… two… *three*!' At the word 'three' Master Johnny flapped his wings and jumped up onto the pig's back… Once he had steadied himself, using his wings and neck, and settled on the bristly back, Master Freddy, with lazy, languid movements and obvious insouciance, as if he was sneeringly dismissing his own prowess, thinking nothing of it, climbed onto the pig's back, scrambled reluctantly up on top of the goose and lingered there, rearing up on his back paws. They had achieved it – what the master called his 'Egyptian Pyramid'. Chestnut squealed with delight, but at that moment the cat yawned, lost his footing and fell off the goose's back. Master Johnny also wobbled, and fell off. The stranger cried out, waved his arms and went off again into long explanations. After a good hour spent on the pyramid, the indefatigable master took it upon himself to teach Master Johnny how to ride on the cat's back, then show the cat how to smoke, and so on, and so on.

The training session came to an end when the master mopped his brow and left the room. Master Freddy gave a snort of disgust, settled down on his mat and closed his eyes, Master Johnny headed for the tray, and the pig was escorted off by the old woman. Given the abundance of new impressions, the day had flashed by unnoticed for Chestnut Girl, who that evening was installed in the box-room along with her mat and the dingy wallpaper, and she spent the night there in the company of Master Freddy and the goose.

5
Talent! Real Talent!

A month went by. Chestnut Girl had got used to being given a delicious dinner every evening and being called 'Auntie'. She had also got used to the stranger and her new flat-mates. Life was flowing by so smoothly.

Every day had begun in the same way. Master Johnny was almost always the first to wake up, and he would come straight over to Auntie or the cat, unwind his long neck and launch forth with passion and conviction on some subject or other, but as always what he said was incomprehensible. Now and then he would hold his head up high and declaim long monologues.

In the first days of their acquaintance, Chestnut had thought that he talked so much because he was highly intelligent, but as time went by she lost all respect for him; when he came up to her with his long speeches, she no longer wagged at him, and she looked on him as a boring old windbag who kept her awake. Unceremoniously she answered him with a 'Grrr…'

Master Freddy, though, was a gentleman of a different order. He was a person who woke up without making a sound or moving a muscle, without even opening his eyes. He would have been just as happy not waking up because one thing was obvious: he was no great lover of being alive. He had no interest in anything; his attitude to all things was one of bland indifference, he was full of disdain, and you could even hear him snorting with disgust as he ate his way through a delicious dinner.

When she woke up, Chestnut would do a walking tour of the rooms, sniffing all the corners. She was alone with the cat in having access to the whole suite of rooms. The goose was barred from crossing the threshold into the room with dingy wallpaper, and Miss Harriet lived outside somewhere in a pen, putting in an appearance only when training was on. The master was a late riser, and once he had had a good drink of tea he got straight down to his tricks. Every day the *pi* construction was wheeled out into the room, out came the whip and the hoops, and every day they ran through virtually the same routine. Training lasted for three or four hours, by which time Master Freddy was more often than not reeling about like a drunk from fatigue, Master Johnny was opening his beak and gasping for breath, and the master was getting red in the face and incapable of wiping the sweat from his brow.

The training and the food made the days very interesting, though the evenings dragged a bit. Most evenings, the master went off somewhere in a carriage, taking the cat and the goose with him. Left alone, Auntie would take to her mat and think sad thoughts... The sadness would steal up on her almost unnoticed, and gradually take over, like darkness coming into a room. It would begin with an awareness that she was a dog who had lost all inclination to bark, eat, run around rooms and even look at things, but then a couple of shadowy figures would appear in her imagination, half-dog, half-human, with nice features, kind but not quite making sense. When they appeared Chestnut would wag her tail, and it was almost as if she had seen them and known them at some time, in some place... And as she dozed off, she would invariably sense that these figures smelt of glue, wood-shavings and varnish.

When she had completely blended in with her new life and been transformed from a skin-and-bone mongrel into a well-fed and cosseted proper dog, one day before the training session the master stroked her coat and spoke to her.

'Auntie, it's time for us to get down to work. You've done enough skiving. I want to turn you into an *artiste* ... Would you like to be an *artiste*?'

And he started to train her in several different ways. In the first session she learned how to stand and walk on her hind legs, which she greatly enjoyed. In the second one she was expected to hop along on her hind legs and grab a sugar-lump held by her trainer high above her head. Then in subsequent sessions she did dancing, circling on a long lead, howling to music, ringing the bell and firing the gun, and before a month was out she had become a capable stand-in for Master Freddy in the Egyptian Pyramid. She was a willing learner, who liked to succeed. She derived the most exquisite pleasure from circling on the lead with her tongue lolling out, jumping through hoops and riding on old Master Freddy's back. Every successful trick she accompanied with a loud yelp of delight, and her amazed trainer, who was no less delighted, ended up rubbing his hands.

'Talent! Real talent!' he said. 'No doubt about it! You're definitely going to be a hit!'

And Auntie got so used to hearing the word 'talent' that when her trainer said it she would jump up and look round as if it was her own nickname.

6

A Restless Night

Auntie had a dog's dream in which she was being chased by a yard-keeper with a broom, and it was fear that woke her up.

The room was quiet, dark and terribly stuffy. Bugs were biting. Auntie had never been afraid of the dark, but this time she felt scared for some reason, and she felt like barking.

In the next room the master gave a deep sigh; a little while later the pig grunted out in her shed, then there was nothing but silence. When you think about food your spirits get a lift, and Auntie turned her mind to the previous day when she had pinched a chicken-leg from the master and hidden it in the drawing-room between the cupboard and the wall, where there was a lot of dust and spiderweb. Not a bad idea to go and have a look, just to check that it's still there in one piece. The master might well have found it and eaten it. But you can't leave the box-room before morning – that's one of the rules. Auntie closed her eyes to get to sleep a bit faster, knowing from experience that the sooner you get to sleep the sooner morning comes. But suddenly, quite near to her, there was a strange cry which made her jump and get up on all four legs. The cry had come from Master Johnny, and it wasn't his usual chatty and confident noise but a wild, piercing, unnatural sound like the squeal of a gate being opened. Seeing nothing in the darkness and greatly puzzled, Auntie felt even more scared, and she growled.

'Grrr…'

A little time went by, about as long as you would need to finish off a nice bone, and the cry didn't come again. Auntie gradually settled down, and dozed off. She dreamt there were two big black dogs, with their haunches and sides covered in clumps of last year's hair, greedily slurping slops from a wooden basin with white steam and a delicious smell rising from it. Now and then they would stop to look round and snarl at Auntie, and growl, 'You're not getting any!' But then a peasant in a fur coat came running out of a house and used a whip to drive them away. Then Auntie went to the basin and tucked into the slops, but the moment the peasant walked out through the gate, both of the black dogs came at her, roaring away, and that was when the piercing cry came again.

'Oooh! Argh!' cried Master Johnny, gagging.

Auntie was now awake, and she jumped to her feet; without leaving her mat she sang out, half-howling, half-barking. She had an idea that it wasn't Master Johnny calling out, but someone else, an intruder. And for no apparent reason the pig gave another grunt out in her little shed.

But then there was shuffling of slippers, and into the room walked the master wearing his dressing-gown and holding a candle. A flickering light jumped about on the dingy wallpaper and across the ceiling, chasing the darkness away. Auntie could see that there weren't any intruders in the room. Master Johnny was sitting on the floor, not asleep. His wings were spread out, and his beak was wide open; he looked exhausted and thirsty. Old Master Freddy was awake too. He must have been woken up by the racket.

'Master Johnny, what's up with you?' the master asked the goose. 'What's all this noise about? Do you feel poorly?'

The goose said nothing. The master felt his neck and stroked his back, and spoke again.

'Funny chap. You can't sleep, and you stop the rest of us sleeping.'

When the master walked out, taking the candle with him, the darkness came back. Auntie was scared. The goose wasn't calling out, but she still had the feeling there was somebody else standing there in the darkness. The scariest thing of all was that she couldn't get her teeth into whoever it was because she couldn't see him, there was nothing to him. And she had an inexplicable feeling that tonight something terrible was going to happen. Master Freddy was upset too. Auntie could hear him tossing and turning on his mat, yawning and shaking his head.

Outside on the street somebody banged on a gate, and the pig grunted in its shed. Auntie whined, stretched her front paws out and laid her head on them. In the darkness and stillness the banging on the gate and a grunt from the pig (why wasn't she asleep?) seemed just as gloomy and scary as the cry from Master Johnny. It was all very frightening and upsetting, but why? Who is that intruder who can't be seen? Then, not far away, two pale-green sparks lit up in a quick flash. It was Master Freddy, making an approach to her for the first time since they had got to know each other. What did he want? Auntie licked his paw, and, without asking what he had come for, she sang out with a soft howl, varying her musical pitch.

'Oooh!' It was Master Johnny, crying. 'Argh!'

Once again the door opened and in came the master with his candle. The goose was sitting there in the same position, with his beak wide open and his wings spread out. His eyes were closed.

'Master Johnny!' said the trainer.

The goose did not stir. The master sat down with him on the floor, looked at him without speaking for a while, and then spoke.

'Master Johnny, what *is* all this? Are you dying – is that what it is? Oh dear, now I remember! Yes, I remember!' he cried out, clapping one hand to the back of his head. 'I know what it's all about! It's that accident yesterday when that horse trod on you. My God, Oh, my God!'

Auntie had no idea what the master had been saying, but she could tell from his face that even he was expecting something terrible to happen. She pushed her snout forward in the direction of the dark window, almost certain that an intruder was looking in at them, and she gave another little howl.

'Auntie, he *is* dying!' said the master. 'That's what it is. Death has come into your room. What are we going to do?'

Ashen-faced and quite distraught, the master went back to his own room, sighing and shaking his head. Auntie felt scared of being left behind in the dark, and she followed him out. He sat on the bed, repeating over and over, 'My God, what are we going to do?'

Auntie walked about round his legs, and, without understanding why, she felt so unhappy and everyone was so upset, she tried to understand it all by following all his movements. Master Freddy, who rarely left his mat, also came into the master's bedroom, and began to rub up against his feet. He kept shaking his head as if he wanted to dislodge any nasty thoughts, and he kept looking suspiciously under the bed.

The master took a saucer, poured out some water from the washstand, and went back to the goose.

'Drink this, Master Johnny!' he said softly, putting the saucer down in front of him. 'Have a drink, old chap.'

But Master Johnny did not stir and did not open his eyes. The master brought his head to the saucer and dipped his beak into the water, but the goose did not drink, his wings just spread out even wider while his head stayed there, lying on the saucer.

'No. There's nothing more we can do!' sighed the master. 'That's it. Master Johnny has gone!'

And shining drops rolled down his cheeks as they roll down windows when it is raining. Without knowing what was wrong, Auntie and Master

Freddy clung to him, looking with horror at the goose.

'Poor old Master Johnny!' said the master with a deep sigh. 'And there was me, dreaming that this spring I would take you out to the cottage and go for walks with you out on the green grass. Dear creature, such a good friend of mine, you are no more! How am I going to manage without you?'

Auntie began to imagine that this would happen to her – one day, without anybody knowing why, she would close her eyes, stretch out her paws and bare her teeth, and everyone would look at her with horror. The same thoughts were obviously going through Master Freddy's head. Never before had the old tomcat been as gloomy and sombre as he was now.

Dawn was coming on and by now the invisible intruder that had given Auntie such a scare had gone from the room. When it was fully daylight the yard-keeper came in, picked the goose up by his feet and took him away. Soon after that the old woman came in and went off with his tray.

Auntie went into the drawing-room and took a look behind the cupboard. The master had not eaten the chicken-leg; it was still there, in the dust and cobwebs. But Auntie felt weary and saddened; she was on the brink of tears. Without so much as a sniff at the chicken-leg, she sat down and began whining in a soft, thin voice.

'Boo-hoo... Boo-hoo...'

7
An Unsuccessful Début

One fine evening the master came into the little room with the dingy wallpaper, rubbed his hands and said, 'Well, then...'

It seemed as if he wanted to speak further, but he didn't do so; he walked out. During her training sessions Auntie had made a careful study of his face and manner of speaking, and she could guess that he was excited, worried and apparently annoyed. It wasn't long before he returned, and spoke to them.

'Today I am taking both of you with me, Auntie and Master Freddy. For the Egyptian Pyramid, Auntie, you are going to stand in for the late Master Johnny. God knows how it will turn out. Nothing's ready, nothing's been properly worked on, we're under-rehearsed. If we flop, we shall drop!'

Then he went out again only to return a minute later wearing his fur coat and top hat. He walked over to the cat, picked him up by his front paws and hid him on his chest under the coat, while Master Freddy showed his total indifference by not even opening his eyes. It obviously made no difference at all to him, lying down or being picked up by the legs, sprawling on his mat or reclining on his master's chest under his coat.

'Come on, Auntie. Let's go,' said the master.

Completely at a loss and wagging her tail, Auntie followed him out. A minute later she was sitting in a sleigh at her master's feet, listening to him as he huddled up against the cold and kept muttering, 'If we flop, we shall drop!'

The sleigh stopped outside a great big house that didn't look quite right – it was like a huge soup bowl turned upside-down. The big wide entrance with its three glass doors was lit up by a dozen bright lamps. The doors sang as they opened like mouths swallowing people who had been swanning around outside. There were plenty of people there, and lots of horses came cantering up to the entrance, but there was no sign of any dogs.

The master picked Auntie up and tucked her away on his chest under his coat, where Master Freddy was already ensconced. It was dark and stuffy in there, but warm. For an instant two pale-green sparks lit up in a quick flash as the cat opened his eyes, disturbed by the cold, hard paws of his new companion. Auntie licked one of his ears, and then, struggling to make herself more at home, she wriggled about awkwardly, crushing him under her cold paws, and inadvertently stuck her head out of the coat, only to dive back inside with a growl of exasperation. She thought she had caught sight of a huge, badly lit room full of monsters. Lurking behind barriers and bars down both sides of the room horrible faces had looked out: faces of horses, ugly mugs with horns or long ears, and a huge, fat one with a tail instead of a nose and two long bare bones sticking out of its mouth.

The cat gave a strangulated miaow from under Auntie's paws, but at that moment the coat was flung open, the master called out, 'Hup!', and the two of them jumped down onto the floor. They were now in a small room with grey boards for walls and nothing in it but a little table with a mirror, a stool and some tattered cloths draped in the corners. Instead of a lamp or candle there was a brightly burning, fan-shaped wall-light fastened to a narrow pipe. Master Freddy groomed his coat, which Auntie had ruffled up, then took himself off under the stool and lay down. The master, still agitated and wringing his hands, started to get undressed. He undressed as he normally did at home when he was getting into bed under his flannelette sheet, stripping down to his underwear, and then he sat down on the stool. With one glance in the mirror he proceeded to do the weirdest things to himself. First, he put on a wig with a parting down the middle and two curls of hair that looked like horns, then he daubed his face with a thick smear of white stuff, and he painted eyebrows, a moustache and red cheeks on top of it. This did not exhaust his fund of crazy ideas. Having made a mess of his face and neck, he began to attire himself in a most unusual costume that looked like nothing on earth – Auntie had never seen anything like it indoors or out. You must imagine the baggiest pair of trousers, made from chintz decorated with large flowers (the kind of material used in low-class homes for curtains and upholstery), trousers buttoned up right under the armpits, with one leg of brown chintz and the other bright yellow. Almost submerged in them, the master then put on a jacket, more chintz, with a gold star on the back, along with a high, pleated collar, stockings that didn't match and green shoes…

Auntie was dazzled in body and soul. This faceless, baggy creature smelt like her master, its voice was also familiar, his, but for minutes on end Auntie had her agonising doubts, and then she was ready to run away from this multicoloured thing and start barking. The new situation, the fan-like lights, the new smells, the master's transformation – all this filled her with a vague feeling of dread and a premonition that she was going to meet up with something horrible like an ugly fat face with a tail where the nose should be. Besides, somewhere through that wall the most ghastly music was being played, and now and then there came a meaningless roar. Only one thing kept her calm – Master Freddy's imperturbable spirit. He was dozing in complete tranquillity under the stool, and he didn't open his eyes even when the stool was moved.

A man in evening dress with a white waistcoat put his head round the door, and spoke to them.

'Miss Arabella is on next. After that it's you.'

No answer came from the master. He pulled out a small suitcase from under the table, sat down and waited. You could tell from his lips and hands that he was worried stiff, and Auntie could sense that even his breathing was nervous.

'And now… *Monsieur George!*' someone called out on the other side of the door.

The master got to his feet, crossed himself three times, picked up the cat from under the stool and put him in the case.

'Auntie, here!' he said softly.

Auntie walked towards his hands without knowing what was going on. He kissed her on the head and put her in alongside Master Freddy. Then – darkness… Auntie stamped all over the cat, scratched at the inside of the case, too scared to make a sound, while the case rocked about and shook like a boat at sea.

'Coming!' yelled the master. 'Coming!'

After this shout Auntie felt the case bump against something solid, and it stopped rocking. There was a loud, echoing roar followed by someone being slapped – that someone, probably the ugly thing with a tail where his nose ought to be, was roaring and guffawing loud enough to shiver the locks on the suitcase. In response to the roar someone shrieked with the kind of laughter that went right through you – it was the master, who never laughed like that when he was at home.

'Aha!' he shouted, trying to make himself heard above the roar. 'Honourable ladies and gentlemen! I've come here straight from the station! My granny's snuffed it and left me a legacy! There's something heavy in this suitcase – must be gold... Aha! I'm about to become a millionaire! Let's open it, and see...'

A lock snapped on the suitcase. Dazzling light hit Auntie straight in the eyes, she leapt out of the case and, with the noise deafening her, she galloped flat out round and round her master, barking at the top of her voice.

'Aha!' shouted the master, 'Good old Uncle Freddy! Auntie, my dear old thing! My beloved family. What the devil are you doing here?'

He threw himself on the sand belly-down, took hold of the cat and Auntie, and gave them a hug. Squashed in his embrace, she managed a quick look at the world into which fate had suddenly plunged her, so shocked by its magnificence that for a moment she froze from amazement and delight, though she soon freed herself from the master's clutches, still wildly impressed and excited, and whirled round like a spinning-top. The new world was huge and brightly lit;

wherever you looked, on every side from floor to ceiling, all you could see were faces, faces and more faces – and nothing else.

'Auntie, please *sit*!' shouted the master.

Remembering the meaning of this, Auntie jumped onto a chair and sat down. She glanced at her master. As always, his eyes looked severe but kind, though his face, especially his mouth and teeth, were hideously twisted into a broad fixed grin. He was chuckling, hopping about and jiggling his shoulders, as if he was thoroughly enjoying himself in front of these thousands of faces. Swept along by his sense of enjoyment, Auntie suddenly felt with every bone in her body that these thousands of faces were looking at her, so she lifted her little foxy muzzle and howled with delight.

'Auntie, *stay*!' said the master. 'Uncle and I want to do a little dance.'

Master Freddy, knowing he would have to do some silly things, stood there glancing nonchalantly in all directions. He put on a feeble performance, too casual, too grumpy, and you could see from his movements, his tail and his whiskers that he thoroughly despised the crowd, the bright lights, the master and himself… He did his bit, then yawned and sat down.

'Now then Auntie,' said the master, 'First off, you and I are going to sing together, and then we'll do some dancing. All right?'

He took a little pipe out of his pocket, and started to play. Auntie, no music-lover, shifted uncomfortably and howled. A roar of approval and applause came from all sides. The master took a bow, and when the noise died down he played on. He was just tackling a particularly high note when somewhere way up in the audience a member of the public gave a loud shout of 'Hey!'

'Daddy,' came a child's voice. 'Look, that's our Chestnut Girl!'

'It is, you know!' The confirmation came from a slightly drunken, tinkling sort of voice in the light tenor register. 'It's Chestnut! *Chestnut!* Fedya, as God's my judge, it's Chestnut!' And he made a whistling sound.

Someone in the gallery had whistled to her, and two voices, a boy's and a man's, were calling.

'Chestnut! Here, Chestnut!'

Auntie jumped, and looked out to where the sound was coming from. Two faces dazzled her just as the bright light had dazzled her before – one of them hairy, drunken and grinning, the other chubby, red-cheeked and anguished… She remembered them, fell off the chair and struggled on the sand, then she jumped up and dived off towards the two faces, yelping with delight. There was a deafening roar cut through by whistles and a piercing child's voice calling out, 'Chestnut Girl! Chestnut!'

Chestnut Girl leapt over the guard-rail and then over somebody's shoulder, ending up in one of the boxes. To get one tier higher she had to jump up over a high wall; she had a go at it, fell short and dropped back, scrambling down. Then she was helped along from hand to hand, licking people's hands and faces, getting higher and higher until she finally made it on to the little gallery…

Another half-an-hour saw her walking down the street behind some people who reeked of glue and varnish. Mr Luke was unsteady on his feet, but, helped along by experience and instinct, was just managing to keep out of the gutter.

'Wallowing in the depths of sin from me mother's womb…' he muttered. 'And you, Chestnut Girl, you'm like a joiner 'longside a cabinet-maker…'

Little Fedya strode along with him, wearing his dad's peaked cap. Chestnut Girl followed on, watching their backs, and soon it was as if she had been following them for ages, and she was so pleased that her life hadn't stopped for a minute.

She still had a memory of the room with the dingy wallpaper, the goose, Master Freddy, delicious dinners, training sessions, the circus. But all of that now came back to her as one long and crazy bad dream.

1887

ELEPHANT AND PUG

Behold the elephant out walking.
He is, of course, on show.
   His kind are all the rage wherever you may go,
   With crowds of people following and gawping.

   From somewhere, suddenly, there comes a little pug,
   Who sees the elephant, and starts to goad and taunt him
With yaps and squeals. Nothing can daunt him:
He wades in, fighting like a thug.

   'Stop!' says a hairy hound. 'I feel embarrassed.
   Why did you have to pick an elephant to harass?
   You're hoarse from barking, but the elephant has gone,
Walked on.
   He never noticed you. He didn't hear you yapping.'

   To which the pug replies, 'Well, as it happens,
   That helps me finish what I have begun.
There'll be no fight, but surely
   I now have been transformed into a bully.
   The dogs will recognise me fully.

   They'll say, "That pug's a hero! Take no chance –
He barks at elephants!"'

I.A. Krylov, 1808

ARTHUR, THE WHITE POODLE
By Arthur Kuprin

1

On the south coast of the Crimean peninsula a little troupe of strolling entertainers was making its way along narrow mountain paths, moving from one settlement of rich men's holiday villas to the next. Most of the time it was Arthur, a white poodle trimmed to look like a lion, who ran on ahead, with his long pink tongue lolling out to one side. He would stop at every crossroads, wag his tail and look back at them quizzically. Following signs known only to him, he never seemed to choose the wrong road, and he would gallop ahead with his ears flapping in delight. The dog was followed by Sergey, a twelve-year-old boy with an acrobat's mat rolled up and tucked under his left arm, while his right hand carried a dirty little cage with a goldfinch in it, trained to dip into a box and pick out coloured slips of paper – messages foretelling the future. Shambling along at the rear came old Martin Lodyzhkin, with a little pipe-organ on his back.

The pipe-organ was an ancient thing that wheezed and coughed like an asthmatic; it had been patched up dozens of times in its day. It only had two tunes: a dreary German waltz by Lanner and a gallop, 'On the Road to China', both big hits thirty or forty years ago and now completely forgotten. There were two broken pipes in it, but grandfather accepted his machine for what it was, and he sometimes said as a joke, though with a suggestion of secret sadness,

'Can't be helped. It's a very old instrument – and it's got a cold. Every time I play it, they people out here on holiday complain about it. "Ugh! What a racket!" And, you know, those tunes used to be nice ones, very popular. Today's gents have no taste for our music any more. Oh, I know about them pipes. I once took it in for a refit – they wouldn't look at it. "Needs new pipes," was all they could say. "Best thing – it's only rubbish – sell it to a museum. They likes antiques." Never mind, it's kept us fed up to now, Sergey, and God willing it'll keep on feeding us.'

Grandad Martin loved his pipe-organ with the kind of affection reserved for a close living being, even a relative. The two of them had grown together over many long, hard years of wandering, and he had come to see it as a spiritual, almost conscious, being.

He had just as much love, perhaps a bit more, for his young companions of the long road, Arthur the poodle and little Sergey. He had 'hired' the lad five years ago from a drunken widowed cobbler, taking him on at two roubles a month. But the cobbler died soon after that, and Sergey was left attached to the old man through ties of affection and the little everyday things they had in common.

2

The path ran along the top of a steep cliff, meandering through the shade of ancient olive trees. The sea flashed into view now and then between the trees. Cicadas chirped incessantly. It was a sultry day with no breath of wind, and the scorching earth burned the feet.

Sergey had been walking ahead of grandfather as usual, but now he stopped and waited for the old man to catch up.

'Something wrong, Sergey?' asked the master of the pipe-organ.

'Phew, it's too hot, grandad. I can't take any more. Be nice to have a dip.'

Without stopping, the old man shifted the organ on his back with a well-practised jerk of his shoulder, and wiped the sweat off his face with his sleeve.

'This is as good as it gets!' he sighed, looking down avidly at the cool blue sea. 'Trouble is, we'd feel worse afterwards. I once knew a field doctor who told me that salt's bad for you. Wears you down – that's what he said. All that salt in the sea…'

'He could have been fibbing,' said Sergey, full of doubt.

'Fibbing? Why should he lie to me? He was a real trooper. Never tasted a drop… He's got a nice little place in Sevastopol. Anyway, there's no way down here. Hang on till we get to Miskhor, then we'll give our sinful bodies a wash. Just before dinner, that's a nice time to have a swim… then you can have a snooze afterwards. Wonderful thing.'

Arthur had got wind of people talking behind him, and he had turned round and run back to them. His mild blue eyes were screwed up against the heat and he looked at them pitifully with his tongue lolling out, trembling from all that panting.

'What's this, little doggie? Bit too hot?' asked the old man.

The dog gave a straining yawn, curled his tongue into a tube, shook himself all over and ended up with a feeble whine.

'Never mind, old chap. Nothing you can do about it. As the good book says, "in the sweat of thy face shalt thou eat bread",' Lodyzhkin went on, sounding like a teacher. 'Not that you've got a face, I mean– more like a muzzle – but still… Go on then, you get out in front. You're under my feet here… But still, Sergey, I must admit I do love a nice warm day. My organ gets in the way. If it wasn't for that, and there was no work on

82

I would lay me down on the grass, in the shade, belly-up and just stay there. Sunshine's the best thing for old bones.'

The path wound down and joined a big highway with a dazzling white, stone-hard surface.

This was the edge of a very old estate that had once belonged to a count, full of lush greenery with a scattering of beautiful holiday villas, flower-beds, conservatories and fountains. Lodyzhkin was very familiar with these places; he did the rounds of them one by one every year at grape-harvest time, when the Crimea is swarming with rich people in their nice togs, enjoying themselves. The old man wasn't much affected by the brightness and richness of the southern countryside, but there was a lot in it that really impressed Sergey, who was here for the first time.

'Hey, grandad, look at that fountain. Golden fish! Wow, grandad, they're made of gold! Strike me dead if they're not,' the boy shouted, pressing his face against the railings of a fence that ran round a garden with a big pool in the middle. 'Grandad, look at them peaches! That lot – all on one tree!'

'Go on, you daft lad. What are you gaping at?' said the old man, nudging him jokily. 'You wait till we get to Novorossisk and head south again. There's places down there really worth looking at. Make you go cross-eyed, they will. Take the palm-tree, for example. Amazing! Got a shaggy trunk rough as matting, you might say, and every single leaf is that big it'll cover you and me both.'

'Honest?'

'You wait. You'll see for yourself when we get there. Anyway, we can't stand here all day tongue-wagging. Get yourself through that little gate. There's some really nice gentryfolk living in this house. You ask me. There's nothing I don't know.'

But it wasn't their day. In one or two places they were sent packing as soon as they appeared on the scene; in others, at the first nasal sounds from the asthmatic organ, they were waved away brusquely from the balcony in great disgust; and there were some where a servant let it be known that 'the honourable master and his lady ain't here yet'. True enough, they did get paid for a performance at two stops, but not much. But grandad was not one to grumble about meagre rewards. As they walked out onto the road he would jingle the coppers in his pocket, looking pleased with himself.

'Two plus five, that's seven kopecks,' he would say with a nice smile. 'Not to be sneezed at, Sergey. Seven by seven, that runs up nearly half a rouble – a decent meal for all three of us, and a night's lodging, and a little noggin for your feeble old grandad Lodyzhkin with all his aches and pains. See, that's what your gentry don't understand! Two kopecks would be an insult, but they would grudge us five... so they send us away. Why not give us *three*? I wouldn't be offended by that. It's neither here nor there... No point in taking offence.'

One way or another the old man, the boy and the dog covered the entire settlement of holiday villas, and now they were ready to walk down to the sea. But there was one more villa, to their left-hand side. It was hidden away behind a big white wall. It was only through a wide pair of iron gates with a wonderfully carved lacy pattern that one could make out a stretch of lawn looking like bright green silk, some circular flower-beds, and, in the far background, a pergola with a thick covering of grapes. A gardener stood in the middle of the lawn, watering roses with a long hose. He had put one finger over the nozzle, and the sweeping spray played with the sunlight in all the colours of the rainbow.

Grandfather was about to move on when he glanced in through the gates and stopped in some surprise.

'Hang on a minute, Sergey,' he called to the boy. 'I think there are some people moving about in there. Funny thing that. I've been going past here donkey's years, and never seen a living soul. Come on, my old mate, tell me what it says.'

'"Friendship Villa. Trespassers Will Be Prosecuted."' Sergey read the sign expertly carved into one of the gateposts.

'Friendship?' echoed the old man, who couldn't read. 'Oh ho! That's a real good word that is, "Friendship". It's not been our day, but now we're going to make up for it. I can smell it like a bloodhound. Arthur, you son of a dog – *ici*! Put your best foot forward, Sergey. I'm the one to ask. There's nothing I don't know.'

3

The garden paths had been evenly scattered with a covering of rough gravel that crunched underfoot, and the borders were made of big pink shells. In front of the house, resting on marble pillars, there were two spheres of mirrored glass, in which the strolling players were depicted upside-down in a weirdly distorted and extended reflection. A terrace with a balcony looked down on a stretch of well-flattened ground. Sergey unrolled his mat on this patch, and Grandad set up his pipe-organ on its pole. He was getting ready to turn the handle when something unexpected and most unusual caught their attention.

A young boy, eight or ten years old, came rocketing out of the inside rooms onto the terrace like an exploding bomb, yelling like a banshee. He was dressed in a light short-sleeved sailor suit which left his knees bare. Blond hair came down to his shoulders in long, loose curls. Half a dozen people came rushing out after him: two women in aprons; a portly old footman in formal dress with no beard or moustache but sporting long, grey side-whiskers; a skinny, red-haired, red-nosed girl in a blue checked dress; a young, sickly-looking but very beautiful lady wearing a lacy, light-blue housecoat; and finally a fat, bald-headed gentleman in a silk suit and gold-rimmed spectacles. They were all in a state of high excitement, flapping their arms, talking in loud voices and even shoving each other about. It didn't take much guessing to see that the cause of all their trouble was the boy in the sailor suit who had suddenly rushed out onto the terrace.

Meanwhile the source of all this turmoil, who never stopped screaming for a second, hurtled on and suddenly flopped down on his belly on the stone floor, spun round onto his back and began to lash out furiously with his arms and legs in all directions. The adults fussed around him. The old footman pressed his hands plaintively against his starched shirt-front, and pleaded with the boy, shaking his long side-whiskers.

'Sir, sir! Master Nikolai! Please don't upset your mummy! Do get up. Drink this, *please*! It's nice medicine, just sugar in water. Please get up.'

The beautiful, sickly-looking lady was moaning with anxiety, pressing a lace handkerchief to her eyes as she spoke.

'Oh, Trilly! For Goodness' sake, Trilly! My angel, I beg of you. Listen to me. Mummy is *begging* you. Please, please take your medicine. You'll see… it'll make you feel so much better… in your tummy and in your head. Just do it for me, my little darling! Listen, Trilly, do you want me to go down on my knees? Look, here I am, down on my knees. Do you want a gold coin from me? Two gold coins? Five? Would you like to have a real live donkey? A real live pony? Oh, doctor, say something to him!'

'Listen, Trilly. Please *be a man*!' boomed the portly gentleman wearing glasses.

'Booh... hoo... oh... ooh... ow... owowow!' yelled the little boy, thrashing around on the terrace floor, and lashing out with his legs in utter despair.

For all his wild agitation he had enough about him to aim good kicks at the stomachs and legs of all the people who were fussing over him, though they were also quite nifty in avoiding them.

Sergey had been watching this scene with a mixture of curiosity and amazement, and now he nudged the old man.

'What's wrong with him, grandad?' he whispered. 'Aren't they going to smack him?'

'Smack him? He's more likely to give them a beating. He's just a spoilt brat. Not too well, either.'

'Gone round the bend, has he?' Sergey ventured.

'How should I know? Shush.'

'Owowow!' screamed the boy, louder and louder, more excruciatingly than ever. 'You horrible pigs! Stupid fools!'

'Start your act, Sergey. I know what to do.' Grandad had taken charge, and he turned the handle purposefully.

The garden rang with the wheezy, nasal sounds and wrong notes of the old-time gallop. Everyone present jumped with surprise, and even the boy stopped screaming for a few seconds.

'Good heavens! As if poor Trilly isn't suffering enough already!' the lady in the light-blue housecoat exclaimed, choking with tears. 'Get rid of these people! Get rid of them right now! And that filthy dog too! Dogs always carry horrible diseases. Ivan, don't just stand there like a statue!'

Raising her handkerchief she waved the performers away with a world-weary expression of disgust; the skinny girl rolled her eyes, and an ominous hiss came from somewhere. The man in formal dress hopped neatly down from the terrace, his face a picture of horror, flung his arms out wide, and ran towards the organ-grinder.

'This is outrageous!' he snorted in an angry whisper that managed to convey suppressed horror with a touch of imperious condescension. 'Who gave you permission? How did you get in? On your way! Move!'

The organ gave a disappointed squawk, and stopped.

'My dear sir, I can explain…' Grandad's tone was the last word in diplomacy.

'Oh no you don't! On your way!' shouted the man in posh clothes, and his words came out in a wheezy, throaty whistling sound.

His fat face had gone suddenly red, and his eyes goggled as if they had left their sockets and come out to rotate. It was so intimidating that grandad stepped back a pace or two.

'Get your things together, Sergey,' he said, rapidly hoisting the organ up onto his back. 'We're off!'

But they had scarcely walked ten paces when piercing cries came again from the terrace.

'Owowow! For me! I want it!… Aaaah! Give it me! Fetch back! Meee!'

'But Trilly… Good gracious, Trilly… But, yes… fetch them back!' groaned the nervous lady. 'You stupid lot! Ivan, can't you hear what's being said to you? Fetch those beggars back. *Now!*'

'Hey! You… what's your name? You with the organ! Come back here!' Sundry voices rang out from the terrace.

The fat footman shot off after the entertainers, bouncing like a big rubber ball, with his whiskers fanning out on either side.

'Hey, listen, you musicians. Come back! Come back!'

'Well, I don't know!' The old man shook his head with a sigh, but he walked back to the terrace wall, took off his pipe-organ, set it up solidly on its post, and started again with the gallop at the point where he had only just been told to stop.

While the wheezy, faltering strains were playing Sergey unrolled his mat, slipped out of his canvas trousers (made from an old sack still bearing the company's square stamp across the beam), discarded his old jacket and appeared before them in his shabby old leotard, much mended but a snug fit for his slim, strong, nimble figure. By carefully watching adult performers he had developed the style of a professional acrobat. He would run out onto the mat, put his fingers to his lips, and then spread his arms in a grand theatrical gesture as if he was sending two kisses streaming out into the audience.

The old man would keep the organ handle turning with one hand, coaxing a wheezing-coughing jingle from it, and use the other one to lob various objects across to the boy, who would catch them all deftly in mid-air. Sergey's repertoire was not large, but he was a smooth performer (having what the experts called 'pure style') and an enthusiast. He could throw a beer bottle up in the air, letting it turn over several times, then catch it bottom-up on the rim of a plate, and keep it balanced for a few seconds. He could juggle with four billiard balls and two candles, which he caught at the same time in two candlesticks. For a finale he would perform somersaults on the mat, run through 'The Frog' and the 'American Knot', and walk on his hands. With his little store of tricks exhausted, he would blow another couple of kisses to the audience, walk over to grandad, getting his breath back, and take over at the organ.

Then it was Arthur's turn. And the dog knew it. He was already excited – jumping up at the old man as he took his strap off, coming at him with all four paws, barking and shivering with anxiety. Who can tell? Maybe the clever poodle was trying to say that in his opinion it was a waste of time doing acrobatics when it was 100 degrees in the shade. But Grandad Lodyzhkin cannily produced from behind his back a thin cherry-wood switch. 'I knew it!' woofed Arthur, expressing his annoyance in one last bark as he slowly and reluctantly stood up on his hind legs without taking his blinking eyes off the master.

'What do you do, Arthur? Yes… Good dog,' said the old man, holding the switch over the poodle's head. 'Now, roll over. That's it. Roll over… Again… Now, let's see you *dance*! Dance, little doggie… Stay! What's that – you don't want to? I'm telling you to *stay*! Look at me… Now, *say hello* to the nice ladies and gentlemen. Look, *Arthur*!' Lodyzhkin raised his voice menacingly.

'Arf!' barked the poodle in distaste. Then he gazed at his master with a pathetic look in his blinking eyes. He had two more things to say: 'Arf! Arf!' This was disgruntled barking with an apparent message: 'My old master doesn't understand me!'

The old man got the dog up on his hind legs, and filled his mouth with the greasy old cap jokingly referred to as his 'top-'at'. Holding on to it, Arthur walked towards the terrace with a mincing, half-squatting walk. A little mother-of-pearl purse flashed in the hands of the sickly lady. Those around her gave a sympathetic smile.

'Hey, what did I tell you?' the old man whispered eagerly, bending down to Sergey. 'I'm the one to ask. There's nothing I don't know. There's at least a rouble in this.'

At this point a shriek of despair came from the terrace, so piercing, so inhuman that Arthur went to pieces, dropped the cap from his mouth, scuttled and skittered away, with his tail down, looking back nervously and finishing up at the feet of his master.

'*Want i-i-i-it!*' bellowed the curly-haired boy, stamping his feet. 'Mine! I want doggeee! Trilly wants doggeee!'

'Goodness gracious! Oh dear! Please, Nikolay... Young sir... Please calm down, Trilly, I beg of you!' Once again the terrace was reduced to turmoil.

'Doggy! Give me the doggy! I wants it! You pigs... horrible devils... stupid fools!' The boy was out of control.

'My darling angel, don't upset yourself.' The lady in the blue house-coat was babbling. 'Would you like to stroke the doggy? That's fine, darling. You can. You can. Doctor, what's your considered opinion – is Trilly allowed to stroke the dog?'

'Normally I wouldn't recommend it.' The doctor spread his hands in dismay. 'But with the right disinfectant – boracic acid perhaps, or a weak solution of carbolic – I, er, I suppose...'

'Doggeee!'

'One moment, darling. Very well, doctor, let's have him scoured with boracic, then... Oh Trilly, don't get so worked up! Old man, would you be so kind as to bring your dog up here? Have no fear. You will be paid. But tell me, he isn't poorly in any way, is he? I mean... he isn't, er, *rabid*? Or... *parasitic*?'

'Not stroking doggee! I won't!' Trilly was roaring, and bubbling at mouth and nose. 'I *wants* doggee! Stupid fools! Horrible devils! Wants to play with him *myself*. Wants him *always*!'

'Listen, old man. Please come here.' She struggled to make herself heard over the racket. 'Oh Trilly, you'll be the death of mummy with all this crying. Why on earth did they let these musicians in? Please, please, come a little closer. We still want a word with you. That's better… Don't cry like that, Trilly. Mummy's going to do anything you want. Please. Do calm him down, miss… Doctor, please… How much do you want, old man?'

The old man doffed his cap. He managed to look deferential and pathetic at the same time.

'Whatever's right according to what your ladyship thinks, your Excellency. We're only little people. Anything we get is a blessing. You'll not do an old man down, I'm sure…'

'Oh, you don't seem to get the point! Trilly, you'll end up with a sore throat… Can't you see – it's *your* dog, not mine. How much do you want for it? Ten? Fifteen? Twenty? Are you with me? Your dog. That dog!'

'Doggee! That doggee!' the boy yelled louder than ever.

This was more than Lodyzhkin could take. He put his cap back on.

'Madam, I am not a dealer in dogs,' he said frigidly, his dignity intact. 'And this dog feeds him and me.' (He pointed back at Sergey over his shoulder with his thumb.) 'He keeps us both in food and drink, and clothing. And there ain't no possible chance of us sellin' 'im.'

Meanwhile Trilly was screeching with all the power of a whistle on a train. He had been given a glass of water, but he had spat it out in his nanny's face.

'But, will you listen, you silly old man? Every object has its price,' said the lady, massaging her own temples with the palms of her hands. 'Miss, do please wipe your face, and fetch my smelling-salts. Maybe your dog is worth a hundred roubles? Two hundred? Three hundred? Answer me, you blockhead! Oh, doctor, for heaven's sake you speak to him!'

'Get your things together, Sergey,' said the old man in a surly growl. 'Blockhead, is it? Arthur. Here boy!'

'Er, wait a moment. There's a good chap,' said the bespectacled doctor in a deep voice full of authority. 'It might be better, my dear fellow, if you didn't get above yourself. That's my advice to you. Ten roubles is a decent price for your dog, and for you too. Don't be a silly ass. Think how much you're getting.'

'My 'umble thanks, good sir, but...' Lodyzhkin gave a grunt as he shouldered the organ. 'But there ain't no way as I would sell, no sir. Might be better to get yourself another dog from somewhere else. I'll bid you good day, Sergey, let's get moving!'

'Are your papers in order?' The doctor was roaring at them ominously. 'I know your kind of riff-raff!'

'Gate-keeper! Semyon! Throw them out!' cried the lady, her face distorted with fury.

The surly gate-keeper in his pink shirt moved threateningly towards the performers. The terrace was pure bedlam, a dreadful clamour of competing voices. But the old man and Sergey had no time to lose; they wouldn't be there to see how it ended. Preceded by a thoroughly chastened poodle, they were heading for the gates almost at running pace. Close behind them came the gate-keeper, harassing the old man with his organ and cursing them with threatening language.

'We've had enough of you layabouts! Damn lucky you've saved your necks this time. You show your face in here again, and I'll have you! I'll grab your collar and get the police in! You scum!'

The old man and the young boy walked on in silence for some time. Then suddenly, as if it had been planned in advance, they looked at each other and burst out laughing. First Sergey began to chuckle, then, glancing at him, Lodyzhkin broke into a slightly constrained smile.

'What about that, grandad Lodyzhkin? I thought there was nothing you didn't know.' Sergey enjoyed his bit of sly teasing.

'You're right, my boy. Went a bit higgledy-piggledy, didn't it?' said the old organ-grinder with a shake of his head. 'Nasty piece of work, that youngster. God knows how they managed to bring him up like that. Just think: two dozen people dancin' round 'im. I tell you what, if 'e was mine, I'd bring 'im into line. "I wants that dog," says 'e. Then what? He's goin' to be askin' for the moon – and can 'e 'ave that? Here, Arthur. Come here, my little pal. Oh well… funny old day! Incredible.'

'This is as good as it gets!' said Sergey with a continuing touch of sarcasm. 'One lady gives us some clothing. Another comes up with a rouble. Nothing you don't know in advance, grandad.'

'That's enough from you, little 'un,' the old man grumbled good-humouredly. 'Remember how you scuttled away from that gate-keeper? Thought I'd never catch you. Mind you, 'e's a tough nut, yon gate-keeper.'

The strolling players left the park, and walked down a steep, crumbling path to the sea. At this point the cliffs fell back a little, leaving a narrow strip of shore covered with even-sized pebbles well polished by the tides, where the sea splashed up with a soft and sweet whispering sound. Less than a quarter of a mile out porpoises could be seen somersaulting, showing their fat, round backs for a moment as they rose from the water.

'We can have a swim here, grandad,' said Sergey firmly. He had already managed to get out of his trousers by hopping from one leg to the other while still walking forwards. 'Let me give you a hand with that organ.' He stripped off quickly, slapping at his bare body, chocolate-brown from the sun, and plunged into the sea, splashing up billows of seething foam.

Grandad took longer to get undressed. Cupping his hand and squinting against the sun, he watched Sergey with affectionate amusement.

'He's coming on nicely,' thought Lodyzhkin. 'He's a bit skinny, you can see his ribs, but that doesn't matter. He's going to be a big strong lad.'

'Hey, Sergey! Don't swim out too far – the porpoises will get you!'

'I'll grab one by its tail!' Sergey yelled from a long way out.

The old man stood there for a while, soaking up the sun, tucking his hands under his armpits. He took his time getting into the water, and before ducking down he wetted his reddening bald crown and his hollow sides. Arthur was barking furiously by now, and racing up and down the shore. He was beside himself, seeing the boy swim so far out. 'Who's he trying to impress with his bravery?' the distraught poodle was thinking. 'There's land here, land for walking on. It's a lot safer.'

Once or twice he had a go at getting into the sea at least up to his belly, and he licked at the water a few times. But he didn't like the salty taste, and the little waves that ran up rustling on the gravel scared him stiff. He soon jumped out, and went back to barking at Sergey. 'Why does he have to perform these foolish tricks? He should be sitting on the shore next to his grandad. Oh, the trouble I have with that boy!'

'Sergey, come on out now. Your time's up!' shouted the old man.

'Coming, grandad! Watch me – I'm a steamer! Pfrrrr!'

At last he swam back to the shore, but before getting dressed he picked Arthur up in his arms, went down to the sea with him and threw him in a long way out. The dog swam straight back, with only his muzzle and his pricked-up ears sticking out of the water, and his loud snorting told of his disgust. Once out on the beach he shook himself from stem to stern, and a shower of spray splashed all over the old man and Sergey.

'Hang on, Sergey,' said Lodyzhkin, staring up the cliff. 'Is he coming our way?'

Hurrying down the path, shouting out something unintelligible, and waving his arms about, came the same surly gatekeeper in his black-spotted pink shirt who only a quarter of an hour before had been chasing the strolling players off the premises.

'What's he after?' asked the old man, nonplussed.

4

The gate-keeper never stopped calling out as he trotted unsteadily down the cliff, with his sleeves flapping in the breeze and his shirt-front billowing out like a sail.

'I say! Would you mind waiting?'

'Get yourself soaked and never dry out!' Lodyzhkin snarled angrily. 'He's come about our Arthur again.'

'Let's give him a pasting, grandad,' was Sergey's valiant proposal.

'You can forget that… But God knows they are funny people.'

'Listen…' The gate-keeper was gasping and still some distance away. 'Would you please sell us the dog? We can't do anything with the young master. He won't stop crying. "Get me doggie. Get me doggie!" The mistress has sent me to buy your dog. The price doesn't matter.'

'Not a very bright thing for your mistress to do,' Lodyzhkin burst out angrily. He felt much more confident here on the shore than he had been at the villa. 'Anyway, she's not my mistress. I don't care what she thinks. So, I'm asking you, please will you go away? For goodness' sake go away and leave us alone!'

But the gate-keeper was not easily put off. He sat down on the rocks next to the old man.

'Listen, you're being very stupid –'

'You're the one who's being stupid,' the old man interrupted, now quite calm.

'Wait a minute, that's not what I'm on about. Don't be so touchy… think about this – it's only a dog. You could get yourself another puppy and teach it to walk on two legs – then, hey presto, you've got a new dog. Haven't you? Am I right? What do you say?'

The old man was busy tightening his belt. He responded to the gate-keeper's insistent questioning with studied indifference.

'Keep going… Then I'll tell you.'

'Well, what matters now, my dear friend, is *the money*!' said the gate-keeper, getting carried away. 'We're talking two hundred, maybe *three* hundred roubles in cash! Admittedly I usually take my own little cut… But just think. Three hundred to go at! You could even set yourself up in a little food-shop…'

As they spoke the gate-keeper took a piece of sausage out of his pocket and threw it to the poodle. Arthur caught it in mid-air, gulped it down, and wagged his tail optimistically.

'Is that it?' asked Lodyzhkin tersely.

'Well, it shouldn't take us long now. Give me the dog, and we'll shake on it.'

'Ri-ight…' said the old man, with a slow, sly grin. 'What you mean is – I've got to sell me dog?'

'Well, it's not that unusual. Just sell it. What more do you want? It's just that our little master's a bit of a handful. If he wants something he can wreck the whole house. You sell – the job's done. When his father's away it's not too bad, but when he's here… praise God and all the saints … everything's upside-down. The master's an engineer. You might have heard of him – Mr Obolyaninov? He's been building railways all over Russia. Worth millions! This is his only son. And he's a devil! He wants a pony, he gets a pony. He wants a boat, he gets a real boat. He's never refused anything. So, how about it, my good man? Have we got a deal?'

The old man had pulled on his brown jacket which had gone green down the seams, and now he sat up as straight and proud as his bent back would allow.

'I've only one thing to say, my lad,' he began, with quite some gravity. 'Take an example. If you had a brother, or maybe a friend, what you had known since you were children – the best friend in the world – *since you were children…* How much would you sell him for?'

'You can't compare that –'

'Yes, you can. You tell your master what goes round building railways, you tell him this: there's things that can be bought that's not for sale. Oh yes. And stop stroking my dog. That won't get you anywhere. Arthur, here boy. Come here, you son of a dog. I'll show you. Sergey, get your things together.'

'You're an old fool,' said the gate-keeper, running out of patience.

'Yes, and I always have been. But you're a sod, you're a Judas, you can be bought,' said Lodyzhkin, cursing. 'You go and see your Mrs General, and you give her my compliments, my love an' my 'umble respects. Roll up your mat, Sergey. Oh dear, me poor old back! We're on our way.'

'So that's the way the land lies,' said the gate-keeper, slowly, meaningfully.

'Dead right,' snapped the old man.

The three performers trudged off uphill along the same coast road. When he chanced to look back, Sergey noticed that the gate-keeper was still watching them. He looked pensive and resentful. He was studiously working away with all his fingers, scratching the back of his red-haired neck from where his cap had travelled down over his eyes.

5

Long before this, old Lodyzhkin had earmarked a pleasant little spot just down from the top road, where one could stop for a nice snack. He took his companions there now.

'Our sins are many, and our food is thin,' said the old man, sitting down in the cool shade of a hazel grove. 'But, Sergey, for what we are about to receive...'

He turned to his canvas bag, and took out a loaf, a dozen red tomatoes, a chunk of Bessarabian cheese and a bottle of olive oil. He also had some salt wrapped in a none-too-clean cloth. After crossing himself several times and with a good deal of whispering he broke the bread into three different-sized pieces, handing the first and biggest to Sergey (a growing lad what needs his food), putting a slightly smaller piece on one side for the poodle, and keeping the third and smallest for himself. 'In the name of the Father and the Son...'

The three of them got stuck into their modest fare, and they did so slowly, steadily and in silence, like real workmen. Nothing could be heard other than three pairs of jaws champing away. Arthur ate his share to one side of them, stretched out on his belly and holding the food between his front paws. When they had had their fill they drank crystal-clear, sweet-tasting water from a tin mug.

'Fancy a quick snooze, boy?' asked the old man. 'I'll just have one last swig of water... Ooh, that's nice! Arthur, here boy!' The old man and the boy lay down side by side in the grass, using their old jackets as pillows. A soft, sweet drowsiness overcame the boy, taking over his body and draining his strength. The old man also dozed off, eventually losing the thread of his favourite after-dinner ideas of a brilliant future for Sergey in some circus. While he was asleep he did once get the impression that Arthur was growling at somebody. For an instant something flashed across his clouded, semi-conscious mind, a memory of the recent gate-keeper in his pink shirt, but, being overwhelmed by sleep, fatigue and all the heat, he couldn't get up; all he could do was keep his eyes closed and send out a lazy call to the dog.

'Arthur, where you goin'? I'll have you, little tramp...'

But these thoughts immediately dissolved and dispersed in a worrying, unshaped, dreamy haze.

It was Sergey's voice that woke the old man. The boy was running up and down the opposite bank of the stream, whistling as loud as he could and calling out at the top of his voice. He looked anxious and afraid.

'Arthur, *ici*! Come back here! Whee! Whee! Whee! Arthur, back here!'

'What's all this shouting about?' The old man spoke automatically while he straightened an arm that had gone to sleep.

'The dog's gone while we were asleep. That's what!' The boy's voice was rough and irritated. 'He's gone!'

'You do have some funny ideas. He'll be back,' said his grandad. Still, he scrambled to his feet, and shouted himself in his old man's reedy falsetto, his voice croaky from sleep.

'Arthur, come back here, you son of a dog!'

He hurried across the bridge, taking short, unsteady steps, and climbed up to road-level, still calling the dog. Before him lay almost a quarter-of-a-mile strip of smooth, dazzling white roadway with nothing to be seen, no shapes, no shadows.

'Ar-thur! Here, boy!' he wailed pathetically. Then suddenly he stopped, bent down to the ground and sat down on his haunches.

'So, that's how it is!' His voice had dropped. 'Sergey, come over here!'

'Why, what have you got?' It was a rude response, but the boy did walk over. 'Have you caught up with yesterday?'

'Sergey, what's happened? You know what's happened, don't you?' The old man's voice was barely audible.

He looked at the boy with a pathetic, lost look in his eyes, and pointed at the ground with a doddery hand. There in the white dust lay a half-eaten piece of sausage, with a scattering of paw-marks all round it.

'That swine's pinched our dog!' whispered grandad, with trepidation in his voice, still squatting on the ground. 'It can't be anybody else. That's obvious... Remember? He was giving the dog sausage when we were down by the sea.'

'Yes, it's obvious,' Sergey repeated in a tone of gloomy bitterness.

The old man's wide-open eyes had suddenly filled with large tears. He blinked them away, and buried his face in his hands.

'Now what, Sergey? Eh? What can we do?' he asked, rocking back and forth, sobbing in his helplessness.

'What can we do?' said Sergey furiously. 'Come on, grandad Lodyzhkin, get on your feet. We're off.' He laid into the old man as if he was a child. 'Stop mucking about. Since when have people been allowed to go about pinching dogs? Don't look at me like that. I'm right, aren't I? We goes in and we says it straight, "Give us our dog back." And if they don't we goes to the court. That's it.'

'No, we can't go to court.'

'Why not? There's one law for everybody. We've got to face up to them.'

'It's my papers. They're not mine.'

'Not yours?'

'They're somebody else's. I lost mine in Taganrog – probably pinched. Then one day in Odessa I was in the doss-house when a Greek chap turned up. "Dead easy," he says, "If you can come up with twenty-five roubles, I'll get you some papers what'll last you a lifetime." Ever since then I've been livin' on somebody else's papers.'

But the boy, white with excitement, suddenly grabbed him under the armpits, encouraging him to get up.

'Come on, grandad! We're on our way,' he said, in a firm but friendly tone. 'To hell with your papers. Let's get going. We can't spend the night out on this road.'

The artistes did not perform again that day. Despite his young years Sergey had a good grasp of what was meant by the fateful word 'papers'. For that reason he didn't insist on searching for Arthur, going to the court or taking any other strong steps. But as he walked along with his grandad to the next doss-house his face remained set, with a new expression of wilful concentration, as if he had had a big idea of real importance. His eyes were directed stubbornly down at the road, and his thin eyebrows were knitted in a dark scowl.

They put up for the night at a Turkish coffee-house with a splendid name: The Star. It was well after midnight when Sergey, who had been lying on the floor next to his grandad, got up carefully and started to get dressed very quietly. Pale moonlight streamed in through the wide windows, painting a slanting diagonal pattern across the floor and then falling on the sleeping figures lined up side by side so that their faces seemed like pictures of suffering and death.

'Vere you goink night-time, you boy?'

It was Ibrahim, the young Turkish owner of the coffee-house, issuing a sleepy challenge at the door.

'Let me out. I've got to go!' answered Sergey in a sharp, businesslike tone. 'Get up, you Turkish clown, now!'

Ibrahim unlocked the door, yawning, scratching and tut-tutting to himself noisily as he did so.

The boy walked past a white mosque with a green onion dome, in a cypress grove that made no sound, and from there down a narrow, winding lane to the highway. Sergey was wearing no top clothes, only the leotard that left him free to move. The moon shone down on his back, and his shadow ran on ahead of him in an oddly foreshortened black silhouette. He was a little frightened by the eerie atmosphere of majestic silence against which his footsteps rang out so clearly and boldly, but at the same time his heart thrilled with a spirit of daring that gave him a light-headed feeling.

He slipped silently into the park through a little wooden gate and walked on into total darkness under the close-set trees. An unsleeping brook murmured in the distance. Then a wooden bridge clattered under his feet, the water beneath it looking black and terrible. At last he came to the big iron gates with their carved lacy pattern, entwined with creeping wisteria. Moonlight cut through the foliage and tinged the carvings with slippery, luminous patches. Beyond that there was nothing but darkness and shivery silence.

It wasn't hard to climb the gate, from where Sergey scrambled up by touch onto a wide stone arch. Lying on his belly, he began to push down on the other side, feeling for a foothold. Fear gripped his heart as his hands went numb, and his weakening body got heavier. Eventually he had to let go. His fingers slipped away from a sharp edge-piece, and he hurtled down.

He heard the coarse gravel crunch under his fall, and felt a sharp pain in both knees. It seemed as if everybody in the villa would be likely to wake up, but no, the silence in the garden was as profound and solemn as before. He got to his feet; the garden was scary and mysterious, a place of fairy-tale beauty. He couldn't recognise things at night, and it took some time to find his way, crunching over the gravel, to the house itself. Never in his life had he felt so helpless and abandoned.

'He won't be in the house… He can't be…' whispered Sergey, as if he was dreaming. 'Keep him inside and he'd be howling. Wouldn't half upset them…'

He walked around the outside of the villa. At the back there was a big yard with less ornate buildings, probably for the staff. Here, as in the main house, there wasn't a single light in any window. Suddenly he could hear something – a thin whine, almost like a moan. The boy stopped, and stood there on tiptoe, holding his breath, his muscles taut. The sound came again. It seemed to come from a stone entry down into a cellar with outside contact through a row of crude, small, square holes with no glass in them. He looked in at one of these vents and gave a whistle. Something stirred, something seemed to have been alerted, but the noise soon stopped.

'Arthur! Artie!' whispered Sergey in a trembling voice.

A terrible racket, one furious bark after another, thundered through the garden, echoing in every corner. He could hear a dog struggling to free itself down there in the dark cellar.

'Arthur! Here! Come on! Artie!' Sergey's voice was choked with tears.

'Blast you. Will you shut up!' came a brutal bass voice from down below.

There was a bang in the cellar. A dog howled.

'Don't you dare hit him, damn you!' Sergey scratched the wall in his frenzy.

What happened then he could only vaguely remember. It seemed like a dream. The cellar door was flung open with a dull thud, and the gate-keeper rushed out, looking to Sergey like a giant, a roaring monster from a fairy tale.

'Who's that? I'll shoot!' His thunderous voice boomed through the garden. 'You burgling swine!'

Next thing, out of the darkness through the open door came Arthur barking and leaping like a bouncy white ball. From his neck dangled a loose bit of string.

Sergey, spring-heeled, ran like the wind, away from the cellar. Arthur was with him, barking with joy as he lolloped along. Somewhere behind them the gate-keeper crashed and banged over the sandy ground, bellowing and swearing.

At the gates the boy realised, more by instinct than calculation, that there was no way over. But between the stone wall and the trees there was a dark, narrow pathway. Without an idea in his head, he panicked, plunged down the path and ran by the wall. Before long the gate-keeper was blundering around all over the place while the boy rushed up and down frantically, several times hurtling past the gates and back into the darkness of the thin track.

Eventually Sergey could take no more. His desperate fear gradually gave way to a cold sensation of weariness and indifference to all danger. He sat down under a tree. But then he noticed something: the wall opposite where he was sitting was quite low, only three or four feet high. The top of it was scattered with broken glass set in lime, but that didn't worry Sergey. In a flash he grabbed Arthur round his chest and lifted his front paws onto the wall. The clever dog knew what to do. He scrambled up onto the wall, wagged his tail, and gave a triumphant bark.

Sergey was soon up there with him, and at that very moment the branches parted and a looming dark apparition peered through. Two nimble figures, boy and dog, jumped smartly down onto the road. A torrent of furious cursing and foul swearing pursued them. It was like being swept away by a muddy stream.

Whether the gate-keeper was less fit than the two friends, or tired out from blundering around the garden, or whether he just realised he couldn't run fast enough, for one reason or another he stopped chasing them. Still, they kept on running; strong and agile, buoyed up by the excitement of escaping, they needed no rest. The poodle quickly regained his usual playful friskiness. Now and then Sergey gave a nervous look back over his shoulder, but Arthur kept galloping round him, shaking his ears and the loose bit of string, and somehow managing to take a running jump and lick him on the lips.

The boy did not come to his proper senses until they got to the spring, the place where he and his grandfather had stopped to eat the previous day. Stooping down together, boy and dog put their mouths to the cool stream and they drank long and thirstily of the pure, sweet water. They jostled against each other and lifted their heads for a moment to get a breath of air, with water dripping from their lips, and then returned to the stream with a new thirst, unable to tear themselves away from it. When, at long last, they fell back from the stream and went on their way, the water splashed and gurgled in their bellies. They were out of danger, the night's horrors had disappeared without trace, and they both skipped along, revelling in their journey down the white road under the bright moonlight between dark shrubs already soaked with morning dew and giving off the sweet scent of leaves with new life in them.

At The Star coffee-house Ibrahim welcomed the boy back with a whispered reproach. 'Vat you do, boy? Vat you go doink? Ah me, iz bad sinks you do…'

Sergey wasn't going to wake his grandfather, but Arthur did it for him. In a split second he had picked out grandad among the sprawling bodies, and before the old man could bring himself round the dog had given a yelp of delight and licked him all over his cheeks, eyes, nose and mouth. Grandad came round properly, and noticed the string round the poodle's neck; he looked down at the boy lying there at his side covered in dust, and he understood. He wanted the details from Sergey, but there was nothing to be had. The lad was fast asleep with his arms flung out and his mouth wide open.

1904

RICH PEASANT AND DOG

There was a peasant once, a man of science,
Who lived in a rich dwelling, self-reliant.
He hired a Dog to stand and guard his yard,
Bake bread, work hard
And weed and water plants when they came into season.

Ridiculous! I tell you flat!
The reader says. *This has no rhyme nor reason.*
Stop teasin'!
  The Dog's on guard – let him do that!
    Have any dogs been known to bake bread – beg your
pardon –
  Or go and water someone's garden?

Reader, it would be slightly out of joint
If I said yes to you, but that is not the point.
The point is this: Barboss took this lot as his target,
Agreeing terms whereby he would be paid for three.
Barboss would get on fine. No help. What need had he?

But then the master rose and took himself to market.
  He drove, he stopped, he strolled. He came back home all
right –
    To see a most unpleasant sight.

He roars with rage, his eyes are swollen.
There is no bread. The plants are stolen,
  And, worst of all, some burgling lout
Has found his store-rooms free, crept in and cleaned them
out.

The guard dog is chastised, but this in turn produces
A backlash from Barboss, who has his own excuses:

     While he was watching plants he couldn't bake the
bread.
     Guarding the yard all day had left him weak-kneed,
aching
    And quite incapable of watching the seed-bed.
    He couldn't look for thieves because, he said,
    He had been busy with his baking.

I.A. Krylov, 1834

ICH BIN FROM HEAD TO FOOT
By Ilf and Petrov

Something stupid, bordering on culpable negligence or worse, has just come to pass.

An act was booked from Germany for a Moscow circus programme: *The Intrepid Captain Masuccio and His Talking Dog, Brünhilde.* (Note: circus captains always have to be intrepid.)

The dog had been booked by the commercial director, an insensitive oaf, who was impervious to modern ways of thinking. And the circus community was dozy enough not to take account of this glaring fact.

They didn't come to their senses until Captain Masuccio set foot on the platform at the Belorussky Station.

A porter came along with a trolley carrying a caged black poodle trimmed in the Louis XIV style, and a suitcase containing the captain's cape with its white Liberty-satin lining and his shiny top-hat.

That very day the cultural committee put the dog through its paces.

The intrepid captain raised his hat a few times, and performed a few bows. Then he put one or two questions to Brünhilde.

'*Wie viel?*' he asked her. ('How many?')

'*Tausend,*' the dog replied, intrepidly. ('Thousand.')

The captain stroked the poodle's astrakhan coat and said with an encouraging intake of breath, 'What a good dog!'

Then the dog pronounced a few words with long pauses between them: *aber … unser … Bruder*, ending with, '*Ich sterbe.*' ('I'm dying.')

It has to be said that at this point there was usually a round of applause. The dog was used to it, and would go along with her master, giving a few bows of her own. But the cultural committee maintained a stolid silence.

And Captain Masuccio, with a nervous look round, proceeded to the end of the act, the climax. He picked up a violin. Brünhilde sat back on her hind legs, waited a bar or two, and then, diffidently and not very clearly, but at full volume, she launched forth.

'*Ich bin von Kopf bis Fuss auf Liebe angestelt.*'

'*Ich bin what*? What was that?' asked the chairman of the cultural committee.

'*Ich bin von Kopf bis Fuss…*' muttered the director of commerce.

'Translation!'

'From head to foot I am made for love.'

'Made for love?' asked the chairman, cutting in, white-faced. 'A dog like that needs a good hiding. This item cannot be allowed.'

Now it was the turn of the director of commerce to go white in the face.

'Why is that? A good hiding?… what for? It's a famous dog going through its repertoire. Big hit all over Europe. What's wrong with that?'

'I'll tell you what's wrong. *The repertoire*. It's middle class, bourgeois, there's nothing edifying in it.'

'Yes, but we've already shelled out, in foreign currency. Not only that – this dog and that man Boccaccio are staying at the Metropole, guzzling caviar. The captain says she can't go on without her caviar. The state has to pay for that too.'

'I'll tell you where we are,' said the chairman, spelling it out. 'In its present form this act cannot go on. The dog has to be given *our* repertoire, in keeping with the times, something progressive. Not this *demobilising* stuff. Think about it! "*Ich sterbe.*" "*Ich liebe.*" Listen, this is a problem about love and death! It's Art for Art's Sake! It's Humanism! It's only a step away from the uncritical assimilation of our classical heritage. No, no, this item has got to be rewritten root and branch.'

'As director of commerce,' said the director of commerce, looking glum, 'I've nothing to do with ideology. But I will say this, as a progressive person working on the front-line of the circus art: don't kill the goose that lays the golden eggs.'

But voting on the creation of a new repertoire for the dog had already taken place. It was unanimously decided to commission a repertoire of the right kind from the in-house minor-matters executive consisting of Usyshkin (aka Verter) and his three brothers: Usyshkin (Vagranka), Usyshkin (Ovich) and Usyshkin (Grandad Murzilka).

The perplexed captain was taken to the Metropole, and told to get some rest.

Special Executive No 6 was not fazed by the request for a dog's repertoire. The brothers nodded in unison without even looking at each other. In fact, it was as if they had spent a lifetime writing for dogs, cats and performing cockroaches. Well, they were veterans of many a battle on the literary front, and they also had the knack of adapting their writing to the demands of working circus ideology at its dourest and most puritanical.

The hard-working house of Usyshkin got straight down to work.

'Maybe we could use the same stuff we wrote for Spider-Woman?' ventured Grandad Murzilka. 'A routine from Saratov that had to fit in with the Circus-Politicisation plan. You remember. Spider-Woman stood for monetary capitalism creeping into the colonies and dominions. Nice act, that one.'

'No, you've not been listening. They don't want bare-faced stupidity. We've got to authorise this dog according to our "Heroic Spirit of Today" plan!' objected Ovich. 'First off, it's got to be written in verse.'

'Can she cope with verse?'

'Not our problem! She'll have to get used to it. She's got a whole week.'

'It must be in verse. Couplets. You know – *Heroic* couplets. About rolling-mills, or else, er – what's it called, that spinning machine? – bankabroche! But the chorus can be a bit lighter, specially written for a dog with a sense of humour. Like this, er … hang on, er … tum-te, tum-te, tum-te … Aha! That's it:

> More shafts and mines and mining stuff.
>> Woof-woof
>> Woof-woof
>> Woof-woof.

'You idiot, Buka!' yelled Verter. 'D'you really think the cultural committee's going to let the dog say, "Woof-woof"? They won't stand that sort of thing. Don't forget the living man behind the dog!'

'Well, it may need changing a bit… De-dee … de-dee … de-dee. That's it. Got it now:

> More shafts and mines and mining stuff.
> Hurrah! Mos-Nav is good enough!

'Deep waters for a dog?'

'Stupid thing to say. *Mos-Nav* is the Moscow Life-saving Association. They don't save lives in shallow waters.'

'Let's drop the poetry. Poetry's just asking for mistakes. It's *doggerel*. That's the trouble with poetry – it narrows the scope. Just when you've got something good to say, a caesura gets in the way, or you can't find a rhyme.'

'Maybe we should give the dog something more conversational? A monologue? Something satirical?'

'I wouldn't. There are hidden dangers there too. What the eye doesn't see, and all that… The whole thing's got to be re-done.'

Brünhilde the talking dog's repertoire met the deadline…

Under the twilit circus dome they came together, all of them – the cultural committee with its full complement and Masuccio in a slightly bloated version, due to his intemperate ingestion of caviar, and a Brünhilde degalvanised from having had nothing to do.

The read-through was conducted by Verter. He did the explaining.

'Ringmaster announces entry of talking dog. Small table covered with cloth brought out. Carafe and hand-bell on table. Brünhilde appears. Needless to say, all your bourgeois frills and fancies – bows and bells and ringlets – they're out. Modest, Tolstoy-style blouse. Canvas briefcase. Dressed in social activist suit. And Brünhilde reads short creative document, only twelve typewritten pages…'

And Verter had just opened his pink mouth to declaim Brünhilde's speech when suddenly Masuccio took a step forward.

'*Wie viel?*' he asked. '*How many* pages?'

'Twelve… in typescript,' answered Grandad Murzilka.

'*Aber*,' said the captain. '*Ich sterbe*. I'm dying. She's only a dog. A *Hund* – know what I mean? She can't manage twelve pages, in typescript. I shall file an objection.'

114

'What's all this? Some kind of self-criticism going on?' asked the chairman with a smirk. 'No, I'm quite clear now. This dog needs a good hiding.'

'*Bruder*,' pleaded Masuccio,' She's still a young *Hund*. She doesn't know it all yet. She wants to. But she can't – not yet.'

'No time for that,' quoth the chairman, 'Let's do without the dog. We'll be one act short. *Volens, nevolens*,[5] you have my con*dolence.*'

At this point even the intrepid captain went white in the face. He called Brünhilde, and left the circus, waving his arms and muttering, 'She's just a little *Hund*. She can't do everything at once…'

The talking dog has now disappeared without trace.

Some say the dog has gone downhill, forgotten how to say her *unser, Bruder* and *aber*. She's turned into a common-or-garden mongrel, and nowadays they call her Polkan.

But these people are whingeing loners, sceptics hiding away at home.

Others have a different story. They say they've got the latest on Brünhilde, who is fit and well, still performing, and a big hit. They even claim that she still knows her old words, and she's got some new ones too. Not quite twelve typed pages, of course, but something to be going on with.

1933

POSTSCRIPT:
THE DOG

There are two of us in the room – my dog and me. Outside a terrible storm is raging.

The dog sits there in front of me, looking me straight in the eye.

And I look back into her eyes.

She seems as if she would like to tell me something. She's dumb, she has no words, she can't understand herself – but I can understand her.

What I understand is that, in this instant, the very same feeling exists in her and in me; there is no difference between us. We are identical: in both of us the same flickering flame burns and shines.

Death will come, flapping his wide, cold wing until… he blows the flame out!

Who then will make out the tiny flame that once burned in both of us?

No, this is not an animal and a human exchanging glances…

It is two pairs of the same eyes, each pair fixed on the other.

And in each of these pairs of eyes, in the animal and the human, one and the same life shrinks down fearfully towards the other.

Ivan Turgenev, *Poems in Prose*, February 1878

Turgenev died in September 1883 at Bougival, near Paris.

His body was taken back to Russia and interred in the Volkov cemetery in St Petersburg.

One of the wreaths that found its way from abroad to be placed on his grave was addressed 'to the author of *Moomoo*'.

It was sent from England by the Royal Society for the Prevention of Cruelty to Animals.

NOTES

1. Minin and Pozharsky were Russian military heroes of the seventeenth century. There is a statue of them in Red Square, and Pozharsky's outstretched arm and hand are enormous.

2. The full Latin phrase is *Caveant consules ne quid detrimenti respublica capiat*, meaning 'Let the consuls take care that the republic is not harmed.'

3. 'I'll take the blame! I'll take all the blame!'

4. 'under my own steam'.

5. 'Willing or not'.

HESPERUS PRESS

Hesperus Press is committed to bringing near what is far – far both in space and time. Works written by the greatest authors, and unjustly neglected or simply little known in the English-speaking world, are made accessible through new translations and a completely fresh editorial approach. Through these classic works, the reader is introduced to the greatest writers from all times and all cultures.

For more information on Hesperus Press, please visit our website: **www.hesperuspress.com**